GOT IT BAD

ALSO BY HP MALLORY:

PARANOMAL WOMEN'S FICTION:
Haven Hollow
Midlife Mermaid
Midlife Spirits

PARANORMAL ROMANCE:
The Underworld Series
Arctic Wolves
Wolves of Valhalla
Lucy Westenra

EPIC FANTASY ROMANCE:
Lily Harper
Dulcie O'Neil
Here to There

PARANORMAL ADVENTURE:
Chasing Demons
Dungeon Raider

REVERSE HAREM:
My Five Kings
Happily Never After

DETECTIVE SCI-FI ROMANCE:
The Alaskan Detective

GOT IT BAD
Book 3 of the EVER DARK ACADEMY Series
By
HP MALLORY

GOT IT BAD

Book 3 of the EVER DARK ACADEMY Series

HP MALLORY

ONE
♀♥♂♂♂♂
Everly

I breathe in the soft scent of pine without opening my eyes.

The scent reminds me of home, of my friends back in the Circle, of *Name Day Ceremonies* from my youth and play-horsing with the other children. The scent brings forth memories of Alivia, my closest friend from the Academy of Divination.

Even now, I can see her spiraling golden hair and rosy apple cheeks. Her pretty plump lips were always stained with some poison berry or another—an example of the fact that she was always chasing the high of mild intoxicants.

I never partook, meaning to keep my body pure as a future High Priestess of the Enclave, and Alivia would always tease me. Yes, Alivia had always smelled of pine. It was as if the tree was woven into the very fibers of her being. No matter the scent of flowers, fragrances, poultices, or perfumes that surrounded her, when Alivia was in the room, you only smelled evergreen.

As I breathe in that scent now, Alivia drifts back into my mind. My chest swells with the sweetly scented air, and my skin prickles, brushed and stroked by the soft beams of sunlight that descend from above. My back is against the ground, and my head rests on what feels like a pile of leaves. I must be in the forest, connected to the spirit and truth of the trees. Though I can't see them around me, I can feel them. Their divine light shines into me, making the sun small and weak by comparison.

My eyes flutter open.

I see my mother's face.

Her long, burgundy hair flows behind her elegantly. She wears her favorite green, backless dress, and her hand is outstretched to me. I reach for it, smiling with my whole heart. It's been so long since I've seen her, since I've looked into those emerald eyes that say with every gaze,

"Welcome home, beloved one."

Just before her hand touches mine, the world goes cold.

She's swept away from me as if by some invisible current. The same force pulls me back, wind in my face and lavender hair flying wildly in front of me, reaching out past the length of my clawing arms.

"Mother!" I cry, but she doesn't hear.

My eyes follow her upward, towards the sky, and she disappears into the blinding light of high noon. Just like that, my happy little paradise is ripped away, and the safety of my mother's company transforms into a hollow, pulsating emptiness in the pit of my gut. My eyes pinch closed again as I claw at the ground, trying desperately to pull myself closer to her, but it's no use. My stomach drops out from under me, and suddenly, I feel a sharp pain in my shoulder, scratching at my skin and pulling me deeper into darkness. The forest around me fades away.

I'm back in my body, but I'm not outside any longer.

I open my eyes and realize I'm exactly where *they* left me, the nauseatingly infantile girl's bedroom in Castle Raven Night—or, at least, I think that's what they called it. For my own part, I can't remember.

In fact, I can't remember a lot of things.

The plush pinks and purples of the decadent space do nothing to comfort me. I look to my left, and the sharp pain instantly stops. I see Riddle withdraw his talons from my shoulder and putter away to his side of the bed, a look of relief in his little yellow eyes. For a bird made of clay and animated by a slice of dryad soul, he's an expressive little guy.

I realize he clawed me to wake me.

Looking around the bed, I see why. The comforter is askew, pushed nearly all the way off the bed, and the pillows are strewn around the room. I reach up to my head and find my hair matted and gnarled by a night of tossing and turning. I must've been thrashing. It probably gave the poor golem the fright of his young life.

"It's okay, Riddle," I say, grateful to the leather-clad incubus for reminding me of the bird's name last night. They were the only words exchanged before the vampire insisted the four of them leave me to my rest.

I still recall the golden eyes of the fire elemental. He looked at me with such intensity; I felt like I might combust under his scrutiny. The vampire gave me a strange look as well—each of them apparently familiar with me in a way I'm not with them. Or, if I am, I can't remember.

The vampire said I lived with him for a time, here in this castle, but I can't find any evidence in my mind to back up the claim. Then again, I can't find much evidence of anything. A forced purging will do that to a girl.

Light beams in through the window. Morning. But it's not the sort of light I'm used to in the town of Blue Water, where I'm from. This light is a pale shadow of that brightness—it's anemic and wan, like the afterthought of light, really. The weak stream of light gray passes through the large window in this bedroom and lights up a quarter of the room. The rest still exists in darkness and cold.

I get up and stretch, hearing my bones pop with stiffness. The sharp snap of something is almost alarming, but it feels undeniably good, a release of tension. And I have tension in spades.

I make my way to the cabinet at the far end of the room. The piece of furniture looks like it belongs in a princess's nursery. It's buttercup yellow with intricately carved patterns of baby blue and decorated with real pink daisies that seem to open and close their petals slightly as I approach. I reach out my hand to one, and it shies away, as if nervous.

Beside the cabinet is a white desk and above the desk are a bunch of random posters of boy bands. I don't recognize any of them, but that means little since I can't remember much of anything. Even though they seem absurd, maybe I'm the one who put them up?

I also can't recall if the armoire of weird looking dolls is mine. Of course, what would an eighteen-year-old girl be doing with a bunch of porcelain dolls that are, at best, expensive-looking and, at worst, the makings for a horror movie?

I turn back to the cabinet with the pink daisies. I slow my reach, taking care to smile and extend my energy to the plant. The petals bend toward me, accepting my touch like a unicorn under the hand of its benevolent master. Touching this flower reminds me of petting Riddle. Both such volatile pieces of magic, and both carrying in them a little bit of someone's soul. I wonder for a moment who it was that enchanted this wardrobe, but then I give up on that thought. For now, I've only got the energy to get dressed. Everything else can wait.

Whatever happened to me, I've gone through a huge ordeal and my body is weak. Not only is my body weak, but there are bruises and cuts all over me. I have a feeling I was in the fight of my life.

Purging, I think the word and ruminate over it for a few more seconds before it begins to make sense to me. *That's what they did to you. They purged you.*

That's right. That's why I feel the way I do— weak and exhausted.

Focus on clothing yourself, Everly, I remind myself, and grab the wooden handle of the cabinet and swing it open. It appears empty from the exposed half. I open the other door, and it reveals more of the same: nothing. I look at Riddle, who raises his wings in a shrug.

Maybe all of my things are still at the Academy dormitory, I think, but my last memories of the Academy of Enchantment are a blur, a confusing tornado of betrayal, pain, and ultimately, salvation—at the hands of men I don't know.

I close the doors again, racking my brain for a solution. It occurs to me then that, just like the outside of the cabinet, the inside must be enchanted. Holding both handles, and keeping the doors closed, I picture what I want to wear. It takes me a fraction of a second to decide. I visualize a knee-length pink dress that reaches my elbows.

I close my eyes, mutter a small incantation for good measure, and open the cabinet again.

There, the dress hovers in the middle of the space, no hanger in sight. I grab it with both hands and, slipping from the white shift nightgown I was dressed in, I pull the pink dress over my head. How I got into the nightie in the first place, I don't recall, but then again, not recalling things is kind of my specialty these days.

Once I'm dressed, Riddle hops onto my shoulder and nuzzles close to my face. It's a comforting gesture, one that feels safe and familiar. I love the feel of his little black feathers brushing against my collar bone, a reminder of a friend and ally who will never leave my side, no matter how confusing things get in my life, or in my dreams. Strange to think that my biggest creature comfort is a creature himself.

"Where to, Riddle?" I ask him, somewhat facetiously. There's nowhere to go. I can't go back to the Academy of Enchantment to finish my training for reasons that are more obvious than Professor Twidly's magically enhanced boobs. I never had Twidly as a teacher at the Academy of Enchantment, but I heard the whispers and saw the evidence: the woman knew *exactly* how to use hormone spells to her advantage.

Thoughts of the Academy of Enchantment cause a heaviness in my stomach, and I swallow hard. If I ever set foot in the place again, I'll be a dead dryad walking. It would've been one thing if the centaur guards of Arcadia had completed the purge and returned me to school, but the men I met in Dread complicated things considerably when they killed so many of my captors. Even so, I find myself grateful to them.

The pain of the purging was like nothing I'd ever known. My blood had turned to liquid fire and was burning my veins, muscles, and tissues from the inside out. I was melting, burning, dying, over and over and over again. Until *they* came for me.

Whoever these men are, I owe them my life.

It's a troublesome thought, not to know the men to whom I'm indebted. And the more I think about it, the more I wonder if I *should* be indebted to them? I mean, yes, on the outside it looks like they freed me, but is that really the case? For all I know, they're a lot of worthless killers who murdered the guards from the land of light for the hell of it and kept me as a souvenir. Afterall, a dryad in Dread is a heck of a sight. It would be like seeing a vampire in the Sacred Circle of my homeland. Shocking. Unnatural, and to some, utterly unacceptable.

So, why am I here? I ask myself. *To be kept as a pet? To be drained of my lifeforce? What could three men of Dread possibly want with a dryad like me?*

No answers come to mind, only more questions. Damn my missing memories!

Riddle rubs the upper flat of his beak against the thoughtful crease in my forehead, and I relax a bit, letting my frown ease. I look at Riddle, not for answers, just for comfort. He nods his massive bird head toward the door. I wonder if it's just a tick or if he's trying to guide me somewhere. In either case, he's the only one in the castle I know I can trust. My memories of the Academy of Enchantment are fuzzy, but I know Riddle stayed by my side. A truly loyal friend. The jury is still out on Harlow, Griim, and the vampire with the name that sounds like demonic royalty.

Something the third... It's on the tip of my tongue.

Following Riddle's silent instructions, I cross the room, open the door, and step out into a chilly and desolate hallway. Sconces with living flames light the stone walls, but the light they offer is overcome by the darkness of the vaulted ceilings and hardwood floors. Everything seems to be a variant of black except for a few pieces of velvet drapery or carpet that are beet red.

Blood red, more likely, I think with distaste.

I walk down the hall with Riddle perched on my shoulder, down a set of spiraling stairs and across another wide expanse, this one looking more like a grand entryway than a hall. Off to the side of the space is a door—slightly ajar—with a modest light peeking onto the floor. A shadow moves beyond the door, then disappears. If I'm quiet, I can hear voices. I look at Riddle and put a finger to my lips.

I take a single step toward the door but stop myself short. Vampires have heightened senses. They can hear heartbeats, breath, or the flutter of an eyelash from what seems like miles away. There's no way I can eavesdrop on that sort of creature without first putting up a guard.

I try to brainstorm spells, all the while feeling a bit guilty at my intent: Dryads are social creatures, but we're also considerate and kind by nature. It isn't our place to steal secrets from shadowy places and keep them for ourselves, nor would any of my kind *want* to do so under ordinary circumstances.

But these aren't ordinary circumstances.

I'm a stranger in a strange land.

And I don't know what's happening to me, where I'm going, what I'm doing, and maybe, most importantly, whether or not I can trust the men who 'saved' me. I've got no choice but to find out the stealthy way.

Finding just the right spell, *Silencing*, I set about casting it with hushed focus. I mouth the little incantation soundlessly, stilling my heart, breath, and body. I close my eyes, complete the spell, and when I open them, I'm hovering an inch or two above the dark floorboards. I focus my energy forward, leaning slightly toward the door, my body hidden by the foreboding black door. There are etchings in the wood that don't look like anything familiar, but they give me an unsettled feeling that starts in my chest and spreads to my extremities. I dare to move an inch closer and listen.

TWO
♀♥♂♂♂♂
Everly

I lean into the door, focusing on the conversation occurring just beyond it.

At first, the voices are muffled, frustrated, but soon enough, rage bubbles over, and the volume increases.

I lean a tad closer to the gap where the door meets its hinge. I place my hand gently against the wall and turn my ear away from the opening and line my right eye up with the narrow slit of light. I can see the three of them. For the first time since I met them last night. Of course, I've been told I've met them all before, but that's just hearsay from men of Dread, hearsay which I must take with the world's largest grain of salt.

"If you think I'm just going to sit around and wait for them to come for her, you're out of your undead mind!"

It's the incubus, Harlow, the one with the leather jacket and the voice as smooth as whiskey.

"Harlow, I know it is quite impossible for you, thus I am, no doubt, wasting my breath, but please attempt to be reasonable," the vampire, Mr. four-names-and-a-number, retorts. "Everly is safe here, and we need to keep it that way. Riven has contacts all throughout Dread. He will be able to help fortify the castle—"

"What, so she can be a sitting duck when the spells break?" Harlow scoffs. "Fuck that. I'm going back and finishing the job. The Academy of Enchantment wants to declare war on us? Let's bring the fucking war to them!"

"You are acting like the petulant child you are," the vampire says.

"Everyone's a child compared to you!" Harlow shoots back. "You're like a trillion years too old to have an opinion that's worth two balls on a satyr. Death doesn't mean shit to you—"

"Everly's does."

I almost gasp, but the spell has stolen my breath, thank God.

The vampire's words seem to shut Harlow up.

The vampire continues, "If you would permit your neanderthal brain a moment to compute, you would swiftly realize I am correct."

"No." A new voice, the fire elemental. I picture his golden eyes staring into mine, and I find myself bizarrely comforted. *Griim*, I recall his name. "You're both wrong. They have an army. The centaurs are practically a military unto themselves. If we leave her here, they *will* come for her, and they *will* kill her." He clears his throat. "At least, that's what I heard them saying back before you rescued us."

"So, what do you suggest, *un fuego*?" Harlow asks sarcastically. "Make a campfire and hope they accept s'mores as a peace offering?"

"We leave," he says. "We take Everly, and we leave."

"And what about the book?" Harlow asks.

Griim shakes his head. "The book is a lost cause. There's no way we can get it when it's in Arcadia."

I don't know what book they're talking about.

"The fireplace is quite correct," the vampire agrees, and Griim shoots him an irritated look.

"So, you think we should run?" Harlow asks, frowning and shaking his head. "And go where? Nowhere is beyond the purview of the Academy of Enchantment. They were the first to stand, and they'll be the last to fall—it's their goddamn motto!"

"I'm aware," Griim says patiently. "But if we wait here, we're sitting ducks, like you said."

"So, we attack them," Harlow says.

"Do that and we will die before we even make it beyond the border," the vampire says. "Besides, according to Riven, they have not formally declared war upon us yet."

"It's just a matter of time," Harlow says. "The damage has been done."

"Perhaps, but perhaps not," the vampire responds. "Riven is doing his damndest to settle the ruffled feathers. And disregarding Granger's dislike for Dread and Ever Dark, he is not going to enter into a war with us lightly."

Granger... Granger... I think to myself, trying to place the name. Then it dawns on me: Headmaster Granger of The Academy of Enchantment.

I hear the vampire release a heavy sigh.

"We will not make any progress until we can all agree on a course of action," the vampire says, his voice cold and distant, as if his thoughts are disconnected entirely from his words.

"No shit," Harlow says. "Unfortunately, 66% percent of us have stupid plans that will get her killed—"

"We may be getting ahead of ourselves," the vampire interjects. "We cannot be certain Everly will be pursued in the first place."

Harlow's scoff blots out the vampire's voice. "You've *got* to be kidding me!"

"Harlow—"

"No, don't *Harlow* me," he shoots back. "She read the fucking book—you heard what Griim said."

"Harlow is right," Griim answers with a clipped nod. "Everly was able to read the secrets in the book, secrets she wasn't supposed to be able to read. And they knew that."

"That means Everly has information and information is costly," Harlow adds.

"The twit makes a good point," the vampire says.

"The twit makes a very good point!" Harlow rages and I wonder if he realizes the vampire was referring to him. "Those bastards *will* come for her, and when they do, not even the great Count Jean-Claude Von Zarovich the *goddamned third* will be able to keep them away from her."

Harlow says the vampire's name with venom, but I'm glad he did. Now I can stop referring to him as "the vampire." My cold former housemate has a name, and it's every bit the mouthful I'd thought it was.

"Count," Griim starts.

The Count ignores Griim and addresses Harlow with the stern resolve of a disappointed school principal. "Though you do make a fine point, you insipid incubus, must I remind you a preemptive strike is a suicide mission?"

"What the hell does that mean in English, dickhead?" Harlow says.

Jean-Claude glares at him. "It means the Academy of Enchantment are prepared for anything the three of us could throw at them."

"You don't know that," Harlow says.

"No, he doesn't, but I do," Griim says. His voice is firmer, imbued with more vehemence than before.

"What the hell are you on about, lava boy?" Harlow snarls.

"I'm the one that went after Everly and found her at the fawn's house," Griim says, his hands tightening into fists at his sides. "When I found her..." He trails off.

There's a moment of silence.

They look more serious than I remember, all of them. Harlow looks angry, forehead creased beneath his slightly wavy brown hair. Griim is pensive and silent still, and Jean-Claude is utterly unreadable, pale skin and dark hair frozen as if etched in marble. Even though I can't remember any of them, one thing I can say about all of them is they're beautiful. The most handsome men I've ever seen. And each is night and day different to the other.

"Speak," Harlow prods Griim like he's a trained dog, but Griim doesn't betray any annoyance. He keeps his cool. Strange, for a fire elemental.

Griim clears his throat and starts again. "Look, I didn't know what I was walking into, but they were coming at Everly from all sides."

"Okay, so what?" Harlow demands.

"That was just to capture her to purge Dread from her system," Griim continues, shaking his head. "Can you imagine the power they'd throw into an attack to avenge their dead soldiers? An attack of retribution for Dread crossing their borders? An attack to get back something they think we've stolen from them?"

"The fire demon is quite right," the count says.

Griim glares at him. "I'm not a demon."

The count waves him away with an uninterested hand. "Fireplace, fire demon… neither are of any consequence to me."

I almost laugh but, luckily, the *Silencing* spell stops me.

Griim looks between the two of them and continues. "Point is—we've broken the rules by coming in unannounced, just like Riven warned. In doing so, we've changed the fabric of the accords."

"The fireplace demon is right," Jean-Claude says as Griim frowns at him. "There is no going back."

"Who's talking about going back?" Harlow asks.

"Were you not just arguing for that point a moment ago?" the count insists.

Harlow shakes his head. "I want to go *forward*. To the Academy. To kill the rest of those bastards before they get to Everly. They think this is war? Then let's give them a fucking war!"

While Harlow is clearly only seeing red and his animated need for revenge is unsettling, a small but mighty voice within me whispers, "you don't need to fear him or them. Your heart knows them well." And I feel the truth of the words, the way I feel the air on my skin, subtle, soft, and entirely without fanfare. Yet, I still can't place their faces. The purging of Dread and all those in it must be made of stronger magic than I've even known. And that's the sticking point because as much as I want to trust them, I'm not sure I should.

I feel a small pang for the Academy of Enchantment. Not because I miss it, of course.

I've never known loneliness and misery like I did at that wretched place. As beautiful as it was on the outside, the facade was blocking out a fiercer darkness than anything Dread could drum up.

My pang for the Academy comes from a younger, simpler version of Everly Stillwater, the version of me who naively believed that the path to High Priestess of my Circle would be simple and seamless, the one who believed the Academy of Enchantment was where she belonged. Oh, how wrong that young little dryad turned out to be.

It's Griim's honeysuckle voice that pulls me out of the sadness that suddenly descends on me.

"By the time you two got to Everly, she'd been poisoned, beaten, burned, and purged, yes, but you didn't see it up close," he says, shaking his head and refusing to look at either of them. "You don't know the reality of what they did to us—"

"What did they do to you?" Jean-Claude asks.

"It doesn't matter," Griim says, quiet but stern.

"If you tell us what happened to you, it might give us a better idea of what happened to Everly," Harlow continues, with some semblance of sympathy or understanding. At least his tone isn't quite so vitriolic.

"Perhaps we should just ask her when she wakes up?" Jean-Claude asks.

"Please don't," Griim says. "Don't make her revisit the pain. It's enough that she's been through it once." He takes a deep breath and shakes his head. "And... they tortured me plenty, but I wasn't purged. Whatever I went through... it doesn't hold a candle to what happened to Everly."

That seems to shut them all up for a while.

I can feel my spell beginning to fade, and I start to sink back toward the ground, slowly but surely, like a gentle hand is pressing me down from above.

"How the hell can you two know what they did to her and *not* want to kill them?" Harlow asks, his tone sending a chill down my spine. There's such hatred in him, hatred I've never seen before. As a dryad, I'm a creature of light. I believe in forgiveness and compassion. There's no time in this life for grudges. Incubi are clearly of a different belief.

"I never said I didn't *want* to kill them," Griim says. "If I could've burned every last one of them alive for what they did to her, I would've done it."

I'm shocked to hear such violent thoughts from Griim. His eyes, though golden with fire, are gentle and kind. There's an intensity about him that overwhelms all his other traits, and when directed toward an enemy, I have to imagine it's just about the most terrifying thing there is.

"I would have drained every last one of those bastards," the Count says, his voice devoid of any inflection, dark and stagnant. "That was never in doubt, incubus."

Harlow stiffens. He clearly doesn't like being referred to by his species. I see him bristle as he folds his arms and leans back against the desk. My toes touch the ground while the rest of me hovers barely an inch from the floor.

What the hell happened to me in all that stolen time? I'm suddenly very lonely for my old memories. Whatever they are, good or bad, they're a part of me, and I desperately want them back, if only to belie my confusion, to explain these creatures and their fascination with whether I live or die.

"Here lies the truth of the matter," Jean-Claude says. "We killed members of their gentry. Many of them. And all to rescue a girl who—by all accounts, including Riven's—was not ours to take. Everly had transferred to the Academy of

Enchantment and that meant she was under *their* protection."

"Yeah, a lot of protection they fucking offered her!" Harlow yells. "They tried to purge us from her memory! All her time in Dread! Her time at Ever Dark!"

"I am well aware, you bestial fool," Jean-Claude spits at him. "My point is that, legally, she was *their* student. By us broaching the accords that exist and entering Arcadia unannounced, we have sanctioned war."

"There hasn't been a battle between Academies in hundreds of years," Griim points out.

Harlow shrugs, looking from Griim to the Count: "Hundreds of years too long, if you ask me."

My spell suddenly breaks, and I drop to the ground. The floorboards creak beneath me, and the men all look toward the door.

"Any chance you've got a house ghost?" Harlow asks.

"Not a ghost," Jean-Claude says. "A guest. Do come in, Everly."

I take a shallow breath and, figuring I've been found out, bashfully walk inside. The scrutiny of their gazes makes me feel like an ant under a child's magnifying glass. I can barely stand it until Jean-Claude finally speaks.

"Gentlemen, leave us."

"Excuse me?" Harlow demands.

"My house, my rules, as they say," Jean-Claude responds. "Griim, you are welcome to leave through the fire."

Harlow mumbles something unintelligible and walking up to me, gives me a nod and a smile. "How are you doing?"

"Same," I answer—as if to say I still don't know who you are and I still don't know if I should trust you.

Harlow nods as if he expects the response, but is still disappointed. "I'll be back tomorrow, Everly." I just nod, not really sure if I should be happy about that statement or not. He looks at me for another few seconds before turning on his heel and leaving the room. I turn to face the others still in attendance and watch as Griim gives me a long thoughtful stare and then, as instructed, steps into the fire that fingers up from the hearth. I'm floored by the sight.

Then it's just Jean-Claude and me and we both stand there for a few seconds, looking at each other but saying nothing. Finally, he breaks the silence.

"Everly," he says. "Did you hear the extent of our conversation?"

"Yes." It's not in my nature to lie.

"I assume you found it... alarming?"

"That's one word for starting a war," I say. "Is all of this really my fault?" I'm terrified of the answer, but my bum memory forces me to ask.

"No," he says.

His handsome face holds such sympathy it's hard to believe he isn't human. His perfect Roman nose and icy black eyes should be intimidating, but I find solace somewhere in their murky depths. The black suit he wears gives him an extra air of authority, and I desperately hope he'll tell me something to quell my confusion.

"None of this is your fault," he says. "If you take away one thing from this encounter, let it be that."

"But there is a war coming?"

"It seems that way," he says, but it doesn't appear his mind is on that subject because he answers the question almost as an aside. "Everly, I must ask you something, and I need the entire truth."

"Okay," I say. The entire truth is all I have to offer to him, and it's owed, considering he may have saved my life. That and he's allowing me to take refuge in his house.

He hesitates. "Do you remember *anything* about me at all?"

Well, that's an easy one. Even so, I don't quite want to deliver the blow. "I'm sorry," I say. "I wish I did."

There's a flash of sorrow on his face, but it's quickly replaced with stony resolve.

"All's well that ends well, I suppose," he says unconvincingly.

"Will it?" I ask shyly. "End well, I mean?"

He doesn't answer, but offers me a pained half-smile.

"I will try most ardently to ensure that it does."

THREE
♀♥♂♂♂♂
Jean-Claude

Everly looks beautiful in her pink frock with her lavender hair flowing behind her as though she walks through the water. I am reminded of the immortal verse of George Gordon, otherwise known as Lord Byron (who was quite a vain twit, let it be known):

She walks in beauty, like the night
Of cloudless climes and starry skies;
And all that's best of dark and bright
Meet in her aspect and her eyes.

I am reminded of the first time I ever laid eyes on the young, vivacious dryad. Even then, she was an orchid among the weeds, the shiniest thing in Dread by a factor of light-years. Her eyes were two perfect moons of opalescent purple, holding me in orbit, a mere meteor in the belt of her influence. And I did feel truly held when those eyes had me in their grip. It was a rare feeling; one I was not certain existed for a creature such as myself.

Then again, those eyes held everyone upon whom their blessed gaze landed. Harlow. Griim. Even Riven was utterly enchanted. Perhaps such was the effect of a life lived in Dread: any glimpse of beauty stood to overwhelm us entirely. Such was and is the effortless power of Everly Stillwater.

"Are you alright?" Everly asks me, nervously tucking a strand of hair behind her pale, delicate ear. "You look... like something isn't right."

I grasp quietly for the proper words, but come up empty. Before I am able to speak, Everly continues, "I'm sorry if... I mean, I don't mean to make you uncomfortable," she mutters quickly, a nervous laugh escaping her luscious lips—no doubt I am staring at her too obviously. "I know it's hard for vampires to be around warm-blooded creatures." It is an odd way to refer to herself, but I stand and listen without interrupting. "I know you're letting me stay here out of your own generosity, and I sincerely apologize if my presence causes you discomfort."

It does.

Cause me discomfort, that is.

But her presence also makes my heart sing as though it were a silly lark. Yes, my heart no longer beats, but when I look at her, I can feel its presence as if it were a breeze blown in from the wind of memory. It is as though the long-dead organ warms and cools in soul-splitting intervals, controlled by the batting of her eyelashes or the intake of her breath.

It is not as though I have never felt such feelings before—I have. Vitrine, one of my own kind, was the original love of my heart and she is also the reason I am the way I am—brooding, antisocial and broken. And, even as I feel the stirrings of that most dangerous weapon located within my chest, I will never allow it full control ever again. I do not believe I would survive its destruction a second time.

Of course, none of that is appropriate to say to a woman who scarcely knows who you are. Everly does not remember me, and thus, the situation must be handled with delicate care.

I keep my eyes on hers and take a few fluid strides forward. She flinches at first, but does not back away. Her stare meets mine with brave tenacity. She is not afraid of an encroaching vampire. More likely, she was afraid of hurting my feelings, attacking my pride. Dryads are people pleasers, and Everly is more pleasing than most.

Once we are standing a mere foot apart, I lift a hand to her cheek and let her flesh warm the palm of my hand. She does not breathe, and I can feel her heartbeat ratchet up a few paces. I revel in the sound. For it is a reminder she is alive. Losing her, finding her, and watching her forget us all—none of that matters when compared to the fact that she is still here, still breathing, still beautiful…

"Do not apologize, Everly," I say. "Not ever."

"But—"

"Just as the sun does not apologize for its glow, and the ocean does not apologize for its vastness, neither shall you apologize for the effect you have on the world around you."

She is speechless for a gratifying moment.

"Count Von Zarovich—"

"Please, call me Jean-Claude."

"Jean-Claude," she starts again with a small smile. It is a pleasure to hear my name on her tongue—in fact, I cannot imagine an opus, a sonata, nor symphony that can compare with the bird-song of her voice. But the lack of recognition in her eyes is gutting, as is her answer to my initial question.

No, she does not recall our time together.

It is as I should have expected, of course, yet the truth stings like the smack of a whip against my undead back.

"I'm so confused," Everly says, eyes downcast. "I don't understand anything that's happening."

"Tell me the last thing you do remember," I command her gently.

Her eyes search the Aubusson area rug of my study—all deep colors woven together to form the shapes of flowers. She fiddles with the hem of her frock and bites her lower lip in fervent thought. One hand brushes her lavender locks away from her forehead. She meets my eyes again and I cannot help but soak in her beauty, careful to disallow my face from betraying my feelings. She does not remember to trust me. That will come with time. Luckily, the one thing I do have is time—in spades. Perhaps my most singular advantage to the others.

"It's all pretty fuzzy," she tells me. "I remember my time at the Academy of Enchantment—all of it, I think. But I don't remember the... book you were talking about."

"The book of Dorian," I say, and she nods. She does not remember the book, for the guards and that bastard sorcerer, Ingram, were sure to purge those memories first, for they were the most important. "Go on."

"I remember Riddle, but the memories with him are hazier than the ones without him. It's almost like… like he's tainted or something."

"The purging was designed to remove Dread entirely from your memory, but it is quite impossible to remove a place's influence fully. Riddle was the wrench in the Academy's plan, a blend of light and dark, and therefore unbanished from both categories."

"Is that why I can't remember any of you?" she asks. "You're all…" She struggles for the last word. "… dark?"

"Indeed," I say. Perhaps I am the darkest of them all. And, yet, perhaps not—mayhap that moniker should be awarded to Riven.

Everly furrows her elegant brow.

"What is the matter, Everly?" I luxuriate in the saying of her name. It is a momentary oasis of peaceful perfection amid the tragicomedy of lost memories of gone away connections.

She laughs, light and lyrical.

"Maybe I should start with what *isn't* the matter?" She whispers to the floor. "It could save us some time." Another soft laugh.

"Time is of no consequence to me," I tell her, feeling the strange stretch of a smile alighting on my lips. I cannot quite help it. I want to comfort her. Somehow. And touching would be inappropriate... and perhaps it would frighten her.

"Right," she says bashfully. "Immortality and all that."

"Yes... and all of that."

Everly goes quiet, thoughtful.

"You can talk to me," I say.

Though I am much better acquainted with darkness, I have learned a great deal about creatures of light in my hundreds of years on this earth. Dryads have a seventh sense about the truth, in general. They are trusting and canny by nature, but equally discerning. I hope she can glean the earnestness of my words.

"I know I can," Everly says, surprising and delighting me in a single swoop.

I gesture to the chair on the far side of my desk, and she takes it without a word.

I sit across from her, stick straight and uncommonly uptight. Considering my nerves have not been active since I was a mortal, this is quite a surprising development.

"Jean-Claude," she starts. "I can't make sense of my life."

"How do you mean?" I ask, though I have a strong hunch.

Everly sighs, the gust of a summer breeze.

"Well, I remember my home in Blue Water and what it felt like to be among my own kind…"

"Yes?"

She swallows, looks into the distance, and sets her mouth in a line, considering the best words to illustrate her point.

"I remember my time at the Academy of Enchantment… for the most part, at least. And I remember how isolated and alone I felt, how… well, just how hopeless I was there."

"What is it you cannot make sense of, then?"

"Well, it's only that… I don't feel that way here," she says with a shrug. "Out of place, or out of step. I feel… I know it's strange to say it, but I feel almost like I remember feeling at—"

"Home."

"Yes," she says, nodding upon a sigh. "Home…"

"I am pleased to hear you are comfortable here." If only she knew how pleased I was and how I have missed her—which is truly saying something because, as a rule, Jean-Claude prefers his solitude.

"But that's what I can't make sense of, Jean," she says.

No one has called me "Jean" since Paris, three hundred years ago. Yes, Annabell—my up-until-recently blood paramour would call me 'Claude' which habitually irritated me. Yet, when Everly calls me 'Jean' now, in the French pronunciation of the word, I do not mind. In fact, I almost prefer it to the courtly nonsense I force on the others. But that is the crux of the matter, is it not? From all others, I must engender fear, intimidation, respect. With Everly, on the contrary, I do not want her obedience or passivity, only her. I do not have to be Count Jean-Claude Von Zarovich the third. I could cease to be all else and be simply... *Jean*.

"I don't remember my time here," she says. "But I can feel this place—it's like it's in my bones," she says with a smile as she looks around her and nods. "Like it's in my blood. It's like the world's worst case of déjà vu."

At the mention of her blood, I feel my canines hum to attention and must force the sudden need to feed from her away. I will not ever take from her unless she asks as much from me pointedly and, even then, I would hesitate.

"But how do I know I can trust you?" she asks as her eyes come to land on me once again. "How do I know you are who you say you are?"

She still carries her doubts regarding Dread, then. It is not a surprising result of the purging, but it a disappointing one, nonetheless. Despite feeling at home here, in Castle Raven Night, she is suspicious of the place as a whole. Of Griim and Harlow. Of me… And I cannot help but understand.

"Unfortunately, there is no way to convince you I am who I say I am." I truly hate to say the next part, but it needs to be said. "And, perhaps even more unfortunately, it does not appear you have any other choice but to learn to trust me… *us*… with time. Just as you did when you first arrived here."

At that, she nods. "Yes," she says softly.

At the open window, a crow lands on the sill. I study it for a moment because, quite bizarrely, its beak is tied shut with twine. Hanging from the twine is a letter. I recognize the stationery at once. I do not need to open the epistle to know what it is: a summons from Riven. Likely, Griim and Harlow have received the same. I look from the bird to Everly and rise from my chair, holding out my arm so the bird can land upon it and I can free its beak.

"Come now, Everly," I say as I gesture towards the door. "There is someone I want you to meet."

"Do I have any choice?" Everly asks, a twinge of sarcasm in her voice.

I smile, despite myself. "That, you do. You may stay at the castle or you may come with me. The choice is yours and I will respect it." And so will Riven, even if I have to force that respect upon him.

I reach out my hand, and she gingerly takes it. The feel of her warmth heats my entire being and I feel myself involuntarily suck in a surprised breath. She looks up at me with those wide and innocent violet eyes and I swallow down my instant hunger as I lead her from the room.

We walk down the far-right staircase (a mirror of the left) to the landing in the middle of the foyer in silence. When we alight the second set of stairs, she looks up at me.

"I am grateful to you, Jean-Claude."

I say nothing but offer her a simple nod and am careful not to squeeze her hand too tightly, as my strength is monumental when compared to hers. I do not want to bruise her.

Stregen, my attendant ghoul, opens one of the double entry doors and Everly studies him as if she remembers him from a dream.

"Come, my dear," I say as I guide her toward Pilot, the Pegasus, and the waiting carriage. Once seated in the carriage, she releases my hand, and it goes preternaturally cold. I long for her warmth but manage to keep as much to myself until we reach Ever Dark Academy.

FOUR
♀♥♂♂♂♂
Jean-Claude

After arriving at Ever Dark Academy, I reach out for Everly's hand to help guide her through the dark stone hallways leading to Riven's office. When we enter, we find Griim and Harlow already awaiting us.

Riddle, Everly's golem familiar, sits on one of her shoulders and, upon seeing the others, squawks out what sounds like a greeting.

On entry, all sets of eyes immediately land on Everly.

Griim's gaze falls to our joined hands. As if just realizing we are still holding hands, Everly readily pulls hers free of my grasp and then looks up at me with an expression of apology. I simply nod. Harlow, meanwhile, stares daggers into the side of my skull. The truant infant is a constant thorn in my side. Riven, as always, looks at us with welcoming crystal eyes alight with the intensity of his curiosity.

I gesture for Everly to further enter the room, and she does without hesitation. This place must hold a sense of familiarity for her just as Castle Raven Night does, purging be damned.

"Everly," Riven says as his eyes land on the lovely dryad. "I am more pleased to see you than you could ever know."

"Thank you," she says nervously, clearly not certain what else to say.

Riven nods. "I've been told you don't remember anything of your time in Dread nor... us." She nods and Riven continues. "I am very sorry to hear it, but please believe me when I say that all of us have nothing but your best interests at heart. We are your protectors."

Everly does not respond other than to simply nod up at him, but I can see in her eyes that she does not fully believe him. There is suspicion there—as it should be. As far as Everly knows, she has never laid eyes on us before.

"Well spoken," I say.

"Count," Riven addresses me with a quick nod. "Thank you for bringing Everly."

I nod in turn and notice with interest that Griim and Harlow have yet to sit. I do believe Riven makes them uncomfortable. Or, perhaps that award goes to Cackus, the dragon superintendent of the academy, who peers out from the blazing fire of the hearth, sternly assessing the room.

A stiff tension crackles through the air and I make my way to the leather club chair beside the fire. I turn to face Everly and beckon her forward.

"Sit," I say as she does and I remain standing behind the chair, leaning over her as I am her foremost protector, no matter where we might be.

"She shouldn't be here for this," Harlow says as he shares his glare between Riven and me.

"Silence, Incubus," I say, narrowing my eyes at the impetuous creature who constantly speaks out of turn. "You have no say in the matter."

He scoffs, crosses his leather clad arms and leans back against a marble pillar. "Oh, Harlow has no say in something? It must be Tuesday!"

"Come off it, Harlow," Griim says. "She'll need to know everything eventually, anyway."

Griim's golden eyes lock on Everly.

Out of my periphery, I watch her look back at him. If my ears do not deceive me, I believe her heart beats a touch quicker, and her breath comes faster, shallower, and less even. The boy's eyes have quite an effect on her. That truth leaves me with a sour taste in my mouth, as though I have just drank the thick, gamey blood of a centaur.

"She will learn everything... that is true enough," Riven says. His spiky brown hair is more askew than usual. He appears as if he has not slept in too long and he is quite emaciated. Furthermore, there are slight but noticeable dark circles underneath his eyes. Were I any less discerning, I would not have noticed, for this difference is a very subtle dimming of his natural aura. Whatever he has to say must be weighing on him heavily.

He straightens his white, ruffled ascot and smooths out the sleeves of his dark green tailcoat, gathering himself to speak. Riven, similarly to me, dresses in the old way—the way of waistcoats, trousers and bowler hats. The way of the gentry, of gentility and high fashion. A way that has, most unfortunately, grown out of favor. Pity that.

Riven has never been one for anxiety, but it is quite obvious that even his nerves are getting the better of him. This unprecedented situation has put us all through the proverbial wringer.

"I'm sure you've all drawn your own conclusions about why I've gathered you here today," he starts.

"Is this an intervention for Count Dick?" Harlow asks upon a chuckle. He turns to me. "We get it. You like sconces," he continues with a shrug as I face him with one elevated brow to show him I do not appreciate his disrespect. "But a hundred-twenty-seven candle holders? That's a bit excessive, dontcha think?"

"Count Dick?" Everly repeats as she looks up at me with wide, surprised eyes, as though she cannot imagine the nerve or tenacity of the ignorant creature.

I shrug in a very unconcerned manner. "That or 'Count Cock'… apparently the incubus is incapable of originality."

"Incapable of originality?" Harlow coughs as his eyes narrow on me. "Let's add 'Count Anus', 'Count Taint' and—"

"Could you be serious for *one* second?" Griim interrupts, turning his irritated gaze on Harlow.

"Gentlemen, please," Riven says, waving his hands in the air as if to say he has had enough. That makes two of us.

"Gentlemen?" I scoff.

We lock eyes, Riven and I. I see the sorrow swimming in their depths, the defeat of a man without options—a man backed against a wall, with a rock and a hard place beating him senseless from either side. He has made a choice that cannot be undone. The truth alights in his eyes.

"It is as I feared, then?" I ask him.

He nods as his gaze rests on Everly again, and it seems he cannot pull it away from her. Riven is just as adoring where Everly is concerned as are the rest of us. Single-handedly, the dryad has wrapped each and every one of us around her proverbial finger, and yet, she does not seem to be aware of the effect she has.

"Super," Harlow says. "So, we're going to war with the cotton candy brigade?"

"Harlow." Griim appears to be losing his patience.

"I didn't say that," Riven answers with a quick shake of his head. "I am still in negotiations with Granger." Then he looks at Everly. "The Headmaster of the Academy of Enchantment."

"I remember who Granger is," she answers in a light voice.

Riven turns to face the rest of us again. "The three of you certainly made an announcement when you went after Everly," he starts.

"And breached the protocol of entry into Arcadia," Cackus finishes as the flames of his fire burn brighter.

Riven adds, "As such, we all bear the responsibility of the broken accords."

"Great," Harlow says.

"Unfortunately, doing so has given Granger the opening he needed," Riven continues.

"Opening?" Everly repeats.

Riven looks at her. "Dread and Arcadia have never been on… good terms," he starts before the incubus interrupts.

"They've just been searching for a reason to try to eradicate us from the planet," Harlow adds.

Riven looks up at him and nods. "And now we've given them one." He inhales deeply. "I believe they will declare war upon us unless…"

"Unless what?" I ask.

Riven turns his forlorn expression to me. "Unless we return… Everly."

Everyone is quiet for a moment or two.

"This is all about me?" Everly asks, as she shakes her head and frowns at each of us in turn. "Why do they care so much about me?"

Riven faces her. "It's not so much that they *care* so about you, Everly," he says, choosing his words carefully. "It's *what you know* that they care about."

"The book?" she asks.

Griim nods. "You have the knowledge of Dorian's journal. You were able to read it and as far as anyone knows, you are the only one with that ability."

"That knowledge frightens Granger," Riven adds.

"But I can't remember any of it!" Everly yells, shaking her head as she throws her hands up into the air.

Riven nods. "That does not seem to matter."

"So what is inside the book that Granger is so freaked out about?" Everly continues. "What did I find out?"

Riven shakes his head. "That's the one-million-dollar question. No one knows." Then he takes in a deep breath and continues as he faces the rest of us. "Because war is most likely going to be the outcome of breaking the accords and refusing to return Everly, I believe we need to start preparing."

"Preparing?" Harlow repeats.

"Wait," Everly says, shaking her head. "If returning me to Granger and the Academy of Enchantment means you could avoid a war with Arcadia, then we all know what you should do."

Riven shakes his head. "No," he answers.

"There's no way I will agree to ever returning you to that awful place," Griim says, his lips tight.

"No, Everly," I say as I look at her and shake my head. "As I said before, we are your protectors."

"So now it's time for plan B, and that plan includes setting up our defenses." Riven nods and faces me. "Jean-Claude, you will gather a brigade of the strongest vampires Ever Dark has to offer."

I nod once, needing no more instruction. If assembling a legion of vampires will help keep Everly safe, I will gladly suffer through the monotony of interaction and, worse still, *student* interaction.

"Harlow," Riven says. "You're our strongest incubus."

"Don't let my brother hear you say that."

Riven nods, but his jaw goes tight at the mention of Lennox, the little bastard. Riven swallows hard. "You'll gather an army of demons and train them in kind... including Lennox, but... I want him kept away from Everly at all costs." He says this last bit in a tone that belies his concern. For as combative and irritating as Harlow is, his brother is worse—unpredictable, quick to anger and generally a waste of flesh. But a *dangerous* waste of flesh.

"You don't have to tell me twice," Harlow answers. "I never planned to introduce Everly to Lennox."

"Very good," Riven says with a curt nod. "You are in charge of assembling and training the demons."

Harlow shrugs and pretends to inspect his fingernails. "I'll check my schedule."

Griim rolls his eyes, lifting his dark eyebrows up to his shaggy hair that always obscures half his face.

Riven looks to Griim, who holds up a silencing hand as if he requires no further orders.

"I'm in charge of training the elementals," Griim says, anticipating the order with a nod. "Not a problem, boss."

"I'm glad to hear it," Riven says, though he looks anything but. The weight of his misery looks downright unbearable, and I can understand why he is so distraught.

War is hell. I have known my share of them.

Men will die.

Alliances will fail.

Families will be torn apart.

I give Riven a small nod of encouragement as if to say, *"Yes, old friend. It will lie heavy on your heart, but you have made the right decision."*

"There's no time to waste," Riven continues. "Two of you will train simultaneously, one brigade on each of our sparring fields. Whoever isn't training will keep an eye on Everly."

"Why do I need *watching*?" Everly asks.

"Not watching," Griim says. "*Protecting*. Granger won't hesitate to come for you, being as—"

"As... this is all my fault?" Everly offers flatly.

"That wasn't what I was going to say," Griim says. "You... you got your hands on Dorian's book." He then looks up at Riven as if to ask permission to continue.

"No one has explained to me, as of yet, just what this book is," Everly says. "And why it's so important."

"It's a book that details the life of an exchange student from Ever Dark to the Academy of Enchantment," Riven explains. "And that book wasn't something the Academy wanted you to see."

"Then how did I get my hands on it?" Everly asks.

Griim shakes his head. "No one knows, but the point is you did."

"And that's why they purged me?" she asks, her eyes going wide with understanding.

"We believe so," Riven answers. "At least, it's one of the reasons." He grows quiet for a moment.

"But we don't believe the purging was complete," Riven answers. "Which means... your memories will return to you... in time. Perhaps not all of them, but it's still a risk the Academy of Enchantment and Arcadia aren't willing to take." He begins to pace the floor before he stands still in front of Everly. "And, on that subject, Everly, I want to request something of you."

"Okay," she says as she looks up at him.

"I want you to try to retrieve Dorian's book," he answers.

Everly immediately frowns. "How am I supposed to do that?"

"With your magic," Riven answers as Everly begins shaking her head, an expression of worry alighting in her features.

"That's impossible," Griim barks out. "The book is still at the Academy of Enchantment."

Riven nods as though he were expecting this argument. "I believe it is possible because I believe Everly shares a connection with the book."

"A connection?" she repeats.

Riven begins pacing the room again. "The book chose to reveal its inner contents to you, Everly," he explains.

"What does that mean?" she asks.

He nods as if expecting her question. "The journal was magicked by its owner, Dorian, and the magick he wove around it disallowed it from being read by anyone in Arcadia. Only someone from Dread would be able to make sense of it." He stops pacing and turns to face her. "And that someone turned out to be you."

"Am I the only person from Dread who could read it?" Everly asks.

"On that topic, I am uncertain, but I would hazard to say yes," Riven answers as he begins pacing again. "But I am fairly convinced that owing to the connection you have to the book, you could retrieve it through your magic."

"What if Granger could track Everly through her connection to the book?" Harlow demands.

"It's too dangerous," Griim agrees.

Before any of us can make another comment, Riddle flies off Everly's shoulder and lands on the floor before the raging hearth. Brandishing his wings on either side of him, he lifts his neck up as high as it will go then bends his head down as his feathers begin to ruffle and a strange coughing sound reverberates through him. A moment later, he opens his beak and a stream of fire shoots out of his mouth, and a book along with it.

"I'll be damned," Riven says as he wears his shock before looking up at me as a smile overtakes his features.

"Is it?" Everly starts before Griim interrupts her.

"The book," he answers on a nod, the shock evident in his tone. "It's Dorian's journal."

Everly looks up at her golem as it flies back to her shoulder, and her smile is beaming. "Good boy, Riddle! Good boy!"

"Who's going to pick it up?" Harlow asks, frowning at the book where it sits upon the floor in a steaming pile of whatever happened to be inside the bird's stomach. It appears to be covered in a slimy goo.

"Quite unsightly," I agree.

Everly gets up from her chair and, leaning over the pile of book and bird-stomach-debris, runs her hand a few inches above it. As soon as she does, the book appears clean, the leather binding still worn but no longer wet with quite repulsive liquid. She picks the book up then and it opens of its own accord. She looks from the book to us.

"Riddle must have swallowed it before we left Arcadia," she says and then nods as she closes her eyes, clutching the book to her chest tightly. "I can see," she starts. "I can see… or I have… I have this image in my mind of Riddle making a nest… yes, making a nest on top of the book."

"If Granger wanted Everly before, he's going to ratchet up his efforts even more so now," Riven says, his tone of voice low. "As soon as he realizes the book is missing, the war will be upon us."

"Alright," Harlow says, pushing himself off the wall. "We've all got our assignments. Who's taking first watch of Everly and the book?"

Griim shakes his head. "Why is he even allowed to talk?"

"Shut it, fire breath," Harlow says. He shoots an arm in the air. "Headmaster Riven?"

"You needn't call me headmaster."

"Would you rather I call you daddy?"

"Wow." Griim's mouth becomes a tight line.

"What is your question, Harlow?" Riven regains control and gives Harlow an unamused, raised-brow expression.

"Not a question," Harlow says. "I'm volunteering. I'll take the first Everly shift."

"How noble of you," Griim says sardonically.

I manage to keep my mouth shut and my fangs hidden.

For now.

FIVE
♀♥♂♂♂♂
Harlow

Count Cock and Griim sneer at me, but I make no effort to hide the smugness on my face.

Since we got Everly back from the land of puppy dog and rainbow unicorn shit, we've all been dying to get some alone time with her. Of course, seeing as how we'd spent the entirety of the night strategizing and arguing among ourselves, none of us had the chance.

Now, here I am, the first to get any real facetime with the lovely dryad. I'm one lucky SOB, if I do say so myself. But I also figure I *should be* the first one to spend some one-on-one time with her because of all of us, I was the closest to her. I knew her the best. Yeah, I'm sure the others would argue with me, but the fact remains.

"Well, you all heard the man," I say, clapping my hands together resolutely. "I'll take *good* care of Everly."

"Yeah, I bet you will," Griim mumbles. His golden eyes are locked on Everly. I follow his gaze and find her already looking at me. There's no trace of recognition in her eyes, but she does appear curious: eyes wide and considering.

"Harlow," Riven says. "Do not take this responsibility lightly."

"Oh, don't worry, bossman," I say without a moment's hesitation. "I'm taking this shit as heavy as possible. Seriously, this thing is like a boulder on my shoulders with how heavily I'm taking it—"

"Will you shut up?" Griim asks, shaking his stupid head. "Seriously, your douchebag routine is like rerun boring."

"Remind me to give a shit, fire breath."

"It's like your parents didn't give you enough attention," Fire Breath continues.

"At least I have parents," I say smugly. Well, as a natural born incubus, I *had* parents at one point, even if I have no idea where those parents are now. Yes, my brother and I were orphaned in Dread from the time we were toddlers. Not that I give much of a shit—I don't. I've learned to rely on myself and make my own way in life. And I wouldn't have it any other way. "You're nothing but animated fire and clay."

"Children," Count Dick says, holding up his hands to silence us. "Enough is bloody well enough."

Riven looks between the two of us and nods. "Jean-Claude is right. There's no need to argue among ourselves. Especially when you'll be relying on each other soon enough."

"Soon enough, as in *how* soon enough?" I ask.

Riven looks pointedly at me. "As in all exits and entrances across all borders into Arcadia and Blue Water have been stopped. Word has spread about Dread breaching the border law and now all counties are preparing, which is why I need all of you to do the same."

"Yeah, yeah." I wave him off. "We get it."

Riven then faces Everly. "And, Everly, I need you to do your part, as well."

"My part?"

"I thought she was just supposed to sit there and look pretty," I answer.

Everyone glares at me then, including Everly. I just shrug and smile as if to say it's not my fault I can't get along with anyone.

"Everly, I want you to try to read as much of Dorian's journal as you can, starting from the beginning," Riven says as Everly nods. "I have a feeling his journal will answer many of our questions."

"And on that fun note, Everly and I are outta here."

"Are you sure Harlow should be looking after her?" I hear Griim ask from behind me. I'm already holding Everly's hand and leading her to the door.

"*I* certainly am not convinced," Count Cock starts.

I hold up my hands. "Hey, what happened to 'we're all in this together' shit? Either we are or we aren't."

"We are," Riven says with a quick nod. "Keep Everly safe and see to it that she gets her reading in."

I look at Griim. His expression is intense but unreadable, giving nothing away. I'm a little disappointed not to have gotten a bigger rise out of him. Maybe I'm losing my touch.

"Right," he says through his teeth.

"Cool, good, awesome, later." Without another word, I take Everly by both shoulders with my gloved hands (without my gloves, she'd probably orgasm right on the spot and I can't imagine that would go over well with this room of buzzkills) and guide her out of the room. The door slams closed behind us, leaving us alone in the empty hallway.

The high, vaulted ceilings let in a few streams of early morning sunlight from outside. Shit, we were stuck in Riven's office for hours if the streaming bits of sunlight are any indication. Not that the light is much—that's because there isn't much light in Dread period. Yet, the rays illuminate Everly's face, dusting light on the tip of her chin, the points of her ears, the silky white of her skin. I give her shoulders a tighter squeeze.

Even now, when she doesn't recognize me, and clearly doesn't remember the kiss we shared a while back, her body's response to mine is instant and gratifying. Her cheeks flush and her eyes go wide. And that gives me an idea. Maybe her mind is having trouble remembering me, but what about her body?

I slide my gloved hands down her arms, and I watch her shiver as gooseflesh covers her. Encouraged, I loop one hand around her waist and pull her next to me.

"What... what are you doing?" she demands.

"I'm... trying something."

"Trying something?"

I nod and with my other hand, I lift her chin up, forcing her eyes to mine.

There's fear in her gaze, but it's expected— desire can be a frightening thing. My desire for Everly sometimes scares the shit out of me. It's doing a damned good job of freaking me out at the moment, actually. I can feel my jeans growing tight in the crotch and my heart is pounding like a war drum. And I haven't even made skin-to-skin contact with her. Yet.

I can hear the sound of Riven, Count Cock and Griim all still arguing in Riven's office, no doubt about me taking first watch—or me taking watch at all. It's no secret that none of them like me. Well, to hell with them—it's not like I like them any better than they like me.

"Close your eyes, Everly." I breathe into her hair and inhale the sweet scent of her.

She stiffens and pulls away slightly. I keep my arm locked around her. She looks down at it with furrowed eyebrows and makes no motion to close her eyes. She doesn't trust me—that much is clear in the depths of her lavender eyes.

"Do you feel it?" I ask.

"Feel what?"

"The way your body remembers mine?" I whisper, nodding in encouragement at her. "Even if your mind doesn't…"

I pull her flush against me and an idea starts to take shape in my mind, solidifying itself. I've held back long enough. Just standing there in that fucking office, trying not to notice her in that tight little dress. It was enough to drive any incubus insane. The fact that I'm not inside her is a testament to my own self-restraint—

"Get off me."

I release her, surprised.

I struggle to find the words. In all the time I've known Everly, she's never had a problem with me touching her. In fact, in the past, she encouraged it. Even if she was and still is a virgin, she was always curious when it came to the two of us. But now that curiosity appears to be missing and in its place is distrust and suspicion.

That purging was a real son of a bitch, I think to myself.

"Sorry," I offer as I cross my arms. The rustling of the leather of my jacket breaks the silence as I lean back to get a look at her. Her face is screwed up in confusion. Her hands are planted firmly on her hips, and there's a look of startled indignation in her eyes. She *really* doesn't remember me.

I'll have to keep that in mind when I'm ripping the human-half clean off a centaur in the coming fight with Arcadia.

"Aren't we supposed to be… going back to Castle Raven Night?" she asks and her voice sounds winded, nervous. She clutches Dorian's journal closer to her chest and Riddle squawks at me. "I need to start reading the book... you heard Riven."

"I'm sorry," I repeat hastily. "It's just that we were... more *familiar* before and I thought maybe I could remind you."

"Familiar?" Everly quirks a dark eyebrow and frowns up at me.

"You never had an issue with me touching you before. In fact, you liked it. A lot."

"I'm just supposed to take your word for that?" she asks, looking at me like I'm the bad guy.

"No," I say. "Take your own word." I'm not even sure what I mean by that and from the look on her face, she's also confused, but whatever. I step closer to her and she inhales sharply, but doesn't step back.

"What... what do you mean?"

I shrug. "Listen to what your body is telling you. Memories of the mind can be tampered with, but the body's memory is infallible." I brush my fingers lightly against her cheeks and she pulls away from me. "You might not know me, but your body knows me..."

A strange look comes across Everly's face.

"What is it?" I ask.

"You say my body knows yours," she says. "Does that mean that... well, did *we* ever... you know?"

"Unfortunately not," I say, chuckling because she sounds like a ten-year-old. Her bashfulness is sweet and dammit all, it's pretty enticing, too. "But I'm pretty sure it was coming."

She rolls her eyes but lets out a small laugh. It's the brightest spot in my day by a mile. "You're *pretty sure*?"

I laugh. "I mean... we liked each other, you know?"

"I don't know—that's the problem." She still eyes me up and down like I'm a thief and she's missing a loaf of bread.

"So, we *weren't* together... sexually?" She asks again, apparently just to make sure. I can't help but wonder if this version of her is even attracted to me. It's just—she acts night and day different to how she used to act around me. It's almost as though... she doesn't even *like* me.

"Not sexually."

"What about dating?"

Hmm, now that's a good question. The truthful thing to say would be, "no, we weren't dating." Technically, no words like that were ever exchanged between us, but we shared a kiss and that felt as good as any declaration. As far as I was concerned, we were as good as on our way to becoming lovers.

"Not exactly," I say reluctantly. "But the fact remains that you were—*are*—very special to me."

"Am I?" she asks, frowning at me.

"More than you know."

She looks down at the ground and breathes out as she shakes her head. "I hate this because none of what you're saying means anything to me. I want to remember, but... I can't. It's just like this big hole where my memories used to be."

"You have no idea how much that sucks for me, too," I say. "But I'm thinking I might have a workaround."

"A workaround?" She looks up. "What do you mean?"

The idea continues to form before my eyes like a statue emerging from a chunk of marble. Once I have it in my head fully, I take her hands again and I wonder if it will work—if I can reinstate her memories simply by accessing the memories of her body.

She rubs her thumb curiously against the back of my hand, feeling the coarse fabric of the black glove. It's the only thing keeping her from the rawness of my desire. I'm reminded of the first time we met when I accidentally touched her. The experience was so overwhelming; I thought I'd never take my gloves off again. Being around her has always been too big a risk, but it's also the sweetest indulgence I've ever known.

"I'm going to help you remember," I say.

She's skeptical and gives me a look. "How are you going to do that?"

"Trust me," I say.

She breathes in deeply and just studies me for a second or two. "Okay."

"Come on."

I pull her toward the slightly ajar stained-glass window at the end of the hall. When we reach it, I push the window all the way up. In response, a gust of wind blows against us, shifting Everly's hair all over the place. Riddle chirps as he tries to maintain his perch on her shoulder.

"What are you doing?" she asks. I don't answer. I just place my hands around her waist and, lifting her up, I turn around to face the window. Riddle flies up and circles us overhead.

"Hold on tight," I say, and as she wraps her arms and legs around me, I leap from the window. She screams, but the sound is like the extended toll of a church bell. We plummet for a few seconds, and I love the feel of the wind whipping against my face, tearing against me as it threatens my life. After another second or so, I release my invisible wings. They catch air a few feet before we hit the ground. Then I swing Everly into my arms, bridal style, and swoop over the forest that separates the school from Castle Raven Night.

"Oh my God…" she says breathlessly as she clutches Dorian's book to her chest, and I hold her even tighter. "I thought we were going to die."

Her eyes are alight with wonder as she takes in the scenery around her.

I smile, a bit smug, and hold her closer.

We arrive at Everly's bedroom window in a matter of minutes. As I float there, my wings flapping to keep me airborne, she reaches out and pulls the double windows open towards us. Then I simply fly into the room and Riddle swirls around my head before flapping to his perch in the corner of her room.

"That was incredible!" she says on an exhilarated laugh as she tries to catch her breath. She walks into her room and lays Dorian's book on her bed.

"You've done it before," I say. "Flown with me, I mean."

"I have?"

I breathe in deeply. "You don't remember?"

She shakes her head and shrugs. "No, I'm... I'm sorry, Harlow."

Damn. So, flying didn't jog her memory the way I thought it might, the way I hoped it might. Maybe another sensory experience will.

My theory is that if Everly's body can experience the same things she experienced here before, in Dread, her associated memories might return. I have a fuck-ton more faith in memory of the physical form than memory of the mind, anyway. And I need Everly to remember me—after everything we've experienced and the feelings we have for each other, I just... she has to.

"Come, sit," I tell her, and she follows me willingly as I lead her to the bed, which is still covered with ridiculous unicorns and hearts. Actually, the whole bedroom looks like it was designed for a seven-year-old girl. You'd think Count Dick would have seen to changing out the bedding, at the least. And the boy band posters? Where the hell he even got those is beyond me.

Since we've just left Riven's office, I figure we have Castle Raven Night to ourselves for another few minutes. Long enough to... try something else. Something a little... more carnal.

I peel off my gloves.

"What are you doing now?" Everly asks, a look of concern washing over her face.

She takes a seat beside me on the bed and I drop the gloves into her lap. She fiddles with the fabric absently, studying each one as if waiting for something to happen. I watch her eyes, looking for a spark of recognition, but I see nothing.

"Everly," I say, turning to face her fully, careful not to touch her. "There's something I can do that I've done to you before that might jog your memory."

"What is it?" she asks.

"It's hard to explain," I say on a shrug. "It's easier if I just show you... may I?" I clear my throat as she looks up at me with those violet eyes—searching my face as if trying to understand if she's safe with me. "It would require touching you... without my glove."

"Will it hurt or something?"

I laugh as I shake my head. "No, but it will be a rush of... exhilaration." I look at her then and let the laugh die on my mouth. "No pain. I promise."

She's still for a moment, then gives me a shy nod. "Okay."

My hand hovers over hers for a moment. I take a deep, shaky breath. She looks at me apprehensively.

"Harlow—"

I grab her wrist with my bare hand, and the two of us are thrust into a world of unceasing and immediate pleasure. I'm welcomed into that special place inside her, that orb of white pulsating light that shines through her skin. She called it the place of her heart before, and I'm pretty sure that's exactly what it is—a halo of warmth and happiness. As the seconds tick by, I find myself dissolving into her essence and the feeling has to be better than any high I've ever experienced.

From somewhere far away, I feel my jeans tightening and that driving desire that tells me to claim her, to make her mine and take from her what I want and need—her essence.

She moans slightly, and her arm shakes in my grasp. Her breath hitches and I can tell her heart is beating fast. So is mine. I move my hand to her leg, just below the hem of her dress, and squeeze. Her skin is so soft and the scent of her—Jesus it's maddening.

"Everly..." I whisper.

"Ah..." is the best she can manage. I move my hand higher up her thigh, and the energy simmering between us is almost too much to bear. She closes her eyes and throws her head back.

"Everly," I say her name again and push her dress up. I want to touch her, want to feel her slick wetness and even though I know I'm going too fast, I can't stop myself.

At the feel of my fingers reaching for her panties, her eyes go wide and she starts to shake her head as she puts her hand on top of mine, where it still sits on the junction of her thigh and torso.

"St... stop..."

The word is like a knife to the gut, but I summon every ounce of my strength and release her, pulling my hand away so I can catch my breath and try to talk the demon inside me down. We both just look at each other for a few seconds, our chests rising and falling with our labored breathing.

"Do you... do you remember... anything?" I manage. I'm panting.

Apparently, she can't speak either because she just shakes her head and appears to be catching her breath.

"Are you telling me..." I say, still panting, "that even after *that* you still don't remember me?"

She shakes her head again, clutching at her heart as if to calm its beat from the outside. "I'm... I'm sorry, Harlow."

"It's fine," I say, not bothering to hide my frustration. Maybe Riven is wrong when he says her memories will start to come back. I mean, if she can't remember this crazy passion between us and her body can't remember it, the purging might have done a more thorough job than we thought.

But I'm not giving up yet.

Leaning forward, I reach up and take a fistful of her hair, holding her head in place as I rotate her chin so her face is level with mine.

"Harlow, what are you—"

She loses the words as soon as I lean down and claim her lips with mine. I don't know how much time goes by as I kiss her—maybe just mere seconds. When she opens her mouth to me, I kiss her harder, deeper. She gasps for air, but I don't give her a reprieve, instead my tongue enters her mouth. And hers suddenly comes forward to meet me. Before I know it, our tongues are mating, tasting each other in a heated dance that makes my body want to follow suit.

I feel my hand land on her thigh again and at the feel of the energy flowing through us, she immediately moans. As she moans, I feel her legs open slightly, welcoming me. I slide my hand up the inside of her thigh. She moans again and I pull my fingers up higher, towards her panties again.

Goddamn do I want to touch her there, to feel her wetness. But if I do...

"No!" She pulls away from me and immediately jumps up, as if I've just burned her. Her expression reveals her distrust as she takes another step away and pants, trying desperately to catch her breath.

"Everly," I start, but she shakes her head and turns to face the window.

"I still... I don't know who you are." She continues to stare at me as if I've upset her. "And whatever *that* was... it did nothing to remind me of anything you and I might have shared together."

Fuck. I don't understand how that can be. How can her body not remember me? Us? Everything we shared? How can she not remember my touch?

Before I have the chance to respond, the door swings open to reveal the fucking vampire. He studies us both for a moment or two as his eyes narrow on me.

"Why is her heart pounding, you bastard?" he demands.

"Because we were trying a little exercise to bring her memories back," I spit the words back as I start for the door. The last thing I want to deal with is Count Cock's inquisition. No, I've had enough for tonight.

"Exercise?" Jean-Claude repeats, his gaze just as piercing.

"Yeah, and it didn't fucking work," I answer as I barge out of the door and down the stairs, all the while trying to come to terms with the fact that Everly doesn't remember anything about me.

SIX

♀♥♂♂♂♂
Jean-Claude

"Everly?" I walk fully into Everly's bedroom as soon as the insipid incubus leaves.

I find her sitting upon the mattress, hugging herself, as tears quietly fall from her lovely eyes. She tries to pat them away, but doing so only accentuates the redness of her heart-shaped face. Instantly, a flood of anger overcomes me and I have a mind to turn around and hunt the bastard down to find out what he's done to her.

"My dear, what has happened?"

Her cheeks color instantly. "Nothing," she says in a small voice.

"Is that blasted incubus to blame for your tears?"

She shakes her head and wipes her sleeve across her eyes. "No," she answers, though I still maintain my doubts. A little hiccup escapes her bowed lips. "I'm just so sick of not understanding what's happening to me."

"Perhaps I can help enlighten you."

She shakes her head and appears slightly distressed by my words. "Harlow… already tried that."

There is something troubling in her tone and, of course, I cannot help but wonder what that useless git has done to her, though I find myself hesitant to ask. My temper, once unleashed, is an unruly thing, and getting it back under control again would certainly be a feat.

"I just want to remember," Everly says, shaking her head as the frustration continues to bleed from her eyes. "It's like a part of my mind's been stolen from me, a whole part of my life… gone…"

"I understand your frustration," I respond. "As it is shared by all of us."

She nods as she looks up at me. "I'm sure you're all frustrated, as well."

I offer her a smile of consolation, though I do not know if the expression provides her the comfort I hope it does. "It is quite painful to look into your eyes and see skepticism rather than trust… I do not blame you for that, of course, but it does not change the truth of the matter, does it?"

"I'm sorry," she says weakly. "I wish Harlow was right."

"Right about what?"

"He seemed to have this idea that my body might have its own memory."

I frown and that deep anger starts to bubble up from within me again. "I fail to understand."

She nods. "His reasoning was that maybe if I felt the same things I did when I was here before, the memories would come back..."

"I have heard more moronic things from the lazy sod, to be certain."

She chuckles slightly at that.

"It was a good enough idea," she continues on a sigh. "But it didn't work when he touched me."

A dark cloud of anger overtakes me as I imagine that good-for-nothing prat touching her, but I keep my reaction in check—at least until I discover more. "He *touched* you?"

She nods and then turns her head toward the window. "It didn't work, though."

"Did he touch you in a way that made you... uncomfortable?" I demand as my hands turn to fists at my sides. One thing I will not allow, especially under my own roof, is for my ward to be assaulted in a way she did not want. I am her protector, after all... And if the incubus touched her in a place she did not want him to—I will rip him into tiny pieces.

She turns to look at me and softly shakes her head. It is then that I detect the scent of desire upon her. Whatever passed between the two of them, she wanted it. And, from what I can tell now, *she still wants it*. Her pheromones are quite... demanding. I am not certain how to feel about that information. On the one hand, I am pleased she was not in some way... debased but, there is another part of me that does not at all appreciate the idea of that incubus spurring her sexual desire for him. I realize, quite guiltily, that I wish for only myself to inspire such feelings within her.

Regardless, we are now entering upon dangerous territory for a female in sexual need is almost impossible for a vampire to deny. Especially when said vampire has an unusual soft spot for said female.

Everly absentmindedly shifts the curtain of her hair back, exposing the long column of her neck and throat. I swallow hard, but I cannot keep my eyes from the bluish pulse at the base of her throat. She catches me staring just before I turn away and will my fangs to return to their usual size.

I must get control of myself. If she sees my animal side, I will undoubtedly frighten her and that is the last thing I wish for. I want her to trust me.

"Were you just... thinking about biting me?" she asks timidly.

After another moment of fighting my inner beast, I turn towards her again and must remind myself of her question. Then I debate whether to be honest with her. In the end, I nod. "I regret to confess I *was* thinking of biting you, though I have been able to wrestle the feeling into obedience on numerous occasions in the past," I say, trying to maintain some semblance of aloof reserve, but I feel vulnerable at admitting the truth of my thoughts, nonetheless.

"Do you think about biting me often?" she asks timidly.

I pause for a moment. "It may very well be what I think about most..."

Everly grows a thoughtful expression on her face—but lacking is any semblance of fear. In fact, the scent of her desire has doubled.

"Please do not be afraid, because I possess extreme willpower," I add, worried this interaction might push her further from me and such is exactly what I most wish to avoid. I want to encourage her trust.

"I'm not afraid," she says.

Though I see proof enough of her words in her expression, I cannot say I fully believe her. I scoff as I respond, "It is okay if you are afraid of me and perhaps... smart, given the fact that I am a predator." I take a pause and penetrate her gaze with my own. "Though I do hope you will believe me when I say I will not hurt you, Everly. Not now. Not ever. When I said I was your protector, I meant every word. No harm will ever befall you when you are with me. Please believe that."

She takes a moment and just looks at me, as though weighing my words and silently trying to figure out what to make of them. There is certainly a semblance of distrust in her gaze, which is to be expected, as I am a dark and mysterious stranger, after all. The purging has left her with no more than a vague impression of having known me, if that. Yet, her blood calls to me. Her body calls to me. And I am fairly sure she feels those facts just as I do.

"What are you thinking about right now?" she asks, and her eyes narrow as she studies my face.

I swallow hard. "I do not believe you would like to know."

She nods her head and does not abandon that fire in her gaze. "I do want to know."

I swallow harder. "I was thinking about your scent—that I can taste your hunger for me in the air."

Her eyebrows raise slightly, as though she is surprised by my verdict. "You can smell it?"

I notice she does not argue her attraction nor desire for me. I find that interesting, though I am uncertain as to why. "Yes," I answer.

Neither of us say anything then—we just simply stare at one another as if we are playing a game of chess and the very next move could make or break the opponent.

"I'm not afraid of you, Jean-Claude," she says at last.

I am elated to hear it, but I keep my expression schooled, betraying nothing. "There is more on your mind, *non*?" I say, only just realizing I have slipped into my native French. I cannot recall a time in recent history when I have done the same. I also cannot recall a time when my feathers were so proverbially ruffled as they are now. This dryad, this woman, has certainly dug her way beneath my skin and as much as that truth shocks me to admit, I must also admit I feel something for her. Something heavy.

Are my feelings for Everly as strong as my feelings for Vitrine, my former lover? I cannot say though I do not believe so. My feelings for Vitrine are another animal altogether—not dissimilar to how Vitrine and Everly, in and of themselves, are night-and-day different. Vitrine was practiced, schooled, a maven in the art of manipulation. Everly is innocence and sweet virtue, understanding and altruism. She is nothing like Vitrine. And, thus, how would it be possible that I should be so inarguably attracted by both?

"I was just thinking that being bitten by a vampire is probably a pretty visceral experience."

"'Visceral' is certainly one word for it."

That thoughtful look intensifies around her eyebrows. I can hear the escalation of her heartbeat, the way her blood starts to pump faster through her body. I can hear the quickened intake of her breaths and smell the added musk in the air.

"Maybe you should..." she starts and then swallows her own words as an expression of apprehension overcomes her features.

I frown. "Maybe I should?"

Then, all at once, the words burst forth as if spewing from a broken dam, "Maybe you should bite me?"

My eyes go perfectly round, and if I had any breath, I am confident it would leave me now.

"You—"

"I know it's a weird thing to ask," she says, nodding as she begins fidgeting with the hemline of her frock, inadvertently pulling it higher up her lovely thighs. "But if *anything* could help me remember you and this place, don't you think it would be your bite?"

The subject does not require any more convincing, even as I know it should. Everly is my ward, my responsibility. Riven gave me explicit instructions when Everly first moved into Castle Raven Night and those instructions were not to seduce her.

And yet… I cannot say *I* am seducing *her*, for I feel it is quite the other way round. The girl is seducing me, but the bloody shocker is I am fairly certain she has no idea what she is doing to me.

I will not harm her, I tell myself, as if searching for some way to justify this request. "You are certain?" I ask, even as my canines begin lengthening and my blood begins boiling within me, calling out to hers, wanting her taste in my mouth.

She nods and exposes her throat, white skin between lavender hair and pink fabric. I bare my fangs and drop my head, inhaling her, tasting her scent. Her breath hitches as I run my finger down the soft skin of her neck and I watch as she pulls her dress higher up her thighs. She wants me to touch her in her most private of places. I do not know if her need is purely brought upon by the incubus and though that subject should concern me, I cannot say it does. Not at the moment, at any rate.

I drop my hand down to her thighs and squeeze her slightly. She responds with a quick intake of breath and puts her hand atop mine. My fangs grace the long column of her neck as her lips part and her breath whistles out. She shifts my hand further up her thigh and closes her eyes.

I am her protector, I tell myself. *I should not take advantage of her.*

Even as the words cross my mind, my fingers reach the apex of her thighs. I feel the soft lace of her panties and I delicately draw my index finger across them. I can feel her heat and her wetness. Her breath hitches and she instinctively pushes her thighs further apart, still encouraging.

My fangs are as long as they have ever been, and the points tease the delicate skin of her neck. I want to bite her. But I know as soon as I do, my urge to feed will overcome me and I will not be able to pay attention to anything else. And I want to pay attention. I want to feel the silkiness of the valley between her legs. I want to experience her wetness, her tightness.

I run two fingers over the top of her panties and she drops her head back against me, a soft moan releasing from her lips. My cock strains my trousers and the need to mate her is almost blinding. Of course, I have had paramours before her—Annabell, most recently. And while I have enjoyed experiencing the inside of many women, the desire and need I have felt for them pales in comparison to this.

I shift Everly's panties to the side and swipe my index finger down her slick sex. She groans out and when I pull my finger away, I see the glistening of her juice upon my finger.

"*Ta beauté est au-delà des mots,*" I speak, the words of my native language coming out before I can stop them. "Your beauty is beyond words," I tell her again, this time in a language she can understand.

She widens her legs, encouraging me to touch her again, and I do. Reaching down, I run my finger up and down her opening, thrilled by her wetness. I center on the sensitive nub of her sex and, rubbing it in tight circles, I watch as her back arches and she grips onto my thigh. Trailing my finger downwards again, I push it into her tight, little opening.

"*Mon Dieu, tu es si serré,*" I whisper, telling her how tight she is.

I push until my knuckle is buried within her and the walls of her channel push against me. I can only imagine what it would feel like to be seated fully within her.

No, focus on her pleasure only, I tell myself.

She pants beneath me, moaning and pushing down as if to encourage me to thrust the entire length of my finger into her.

"Bite me, please," she whispers.

My fangs are still perched at her throat. And, as I pull my finger from her folds and replace it with two, I break the seal of her throat with my fangs as I thrust both fingers into her at the same time.

The first rush of Everly's blood touches my tongue at the same moment that her body shakes and an orgasm seizes her.

I am undone.

Her blood is more than a flavor. It is a feeling. The feeling of Everly—the touch of her, the smell of her, the feel of her. The *experience* of her. I drink fervently, grasping her throat with my free hand to steady myself, to keep myself from falling forward. I continue to thrust my finger inside and out of her, mating her with my hand even though I desire nothing more than to truly mate her. But that cannot be. Not yet anyway.

As I suck at the wound of her throat, she continues to moan, and the sound only spurs me on. Her body begins to ripple with another orgasm and then she reaches down, pushing my fingers from her drenched opening.

"Jean-Claude…" she says on a weak breath. "No more."

I gather all the resolve in my body and pull my fangs from her, looking into her eyes as I lick the last of her blood from my canines.

We stare at one another as we gather ourselves—she pulling her panties back into place and replacing her frock over her thighs while a blush creeps over her cheeks.

I see, there in her gaze, everything I need to know: despite the raw emotion we exchanged, she still does not remember.

"There's nothing there," she says sadly as she reaches up and fingers the small fang marks in her throat. "I still can't remember anything."

"Everly," I start, but she shakes her head and pulls away from me. Before she does, I see the water in her eyes.

"I... I need to be alone," she says.

She jumps up then and retreats to the door. Then she hurries down the hall and heads straight into the woods I created for her...

SEVEN
♀♥♂♂♂♂
Griim

Harlow forfeited his chance to watch Everly, because he couldn't deal with the fact that she can't remember him.

So, I decided to take his watch.

And now, as I walk up the winding staircase to her bedroom, I can't help noticing the whimpers and soft moans that fill the air. At first, I believe she's in trouble, but the more I listen, the more I realize they aren't moans of fear—they're moans of passion.

Skulking in the shadows, I listen as the count speaks to her in his native French language and she moans in response. I don't believe they're having sex, because I can't hear any creaks from the bed. Fascinated, I remain in the shadows, listening.

When footsteps sound in my direction, I skulk back into the shadows, hiding. I watch Everly leave her bedroom and then hurry down the stairs. She's upset.

I'm not sure if I should follow her to see if I can find out why. Then I decide it would be better to face the count and find out what's just happened and if the bastard has taken liberties with her that he shouldn't have. Her protector, my ass.

If he's hurt her… I don't know what I'll do. I'll want to tear his head off, but that's not a possibility, considering how much stronger he is than me.

Waiting another few seconds, I walk into her bedroom, where Jean-Claude still sits on her bed. His expression is a guilty one as he looks up at me.

"Where is she?" I ask, frowning at him.

"The woods," he says. It's then I notice the dribble of crimson blood on his chin.

A flash of fury overwhelms me and I have to take a few breaths to calm myself, even as I feel like attacking him. But attacking the oldest of the vampires isn't a good move. No, it's a really stupid move. He could have my head in a second.

Of course, Cackus could reanimate me, but that's not a situation I want to experience anytime soon. Better to play this the safe way.

I take another moment to compose myself.

"No doubt you have noticed the blood on my face," Jean-Claude says as he looks up and his eyes meet mine.

"You were feeding on her?" I ask quietly, my voice barely held in check.

"I nibbled, yes."

"When you were supposed to be protecting her?"

"Asking questions for which you really do not want to know the answer is a bad habit most people have," he says.

That's all the confirmation I need.

Breathing in deeply, I turn around and start for the stairs, headed for the woods. Hopefully Everly hasn't gone too far, but by the fact that she left the castle and Jean-Claude is still sitting in her bedroom, I can't imagine the situation between them was a good one.

"Everly!" I cup my hands around my mouth and shout her name when I reach the mouth of the forest. My voice does nothing but echo back to me against the seemingly endless tree line. "Everly!"

I don't get an answer.

I continue further into the forest and after another ten or so paces, I hear a sound—a slight, pittering. The sound turns into a rhythmic thumping, and I follow in silent pursuit. As I travel deeper into the forest, the sound grows louder. After a few minutes of running, the sound is all but deafening and moments later, I stumble on the source. The sounds become layered with lyrical incantations.

These are the notes of a spell.

I round a tall elm and catch sight of a flurry of lavender hair.

And there she is, looking radiant, bathed in a circle of light of her own creation.

"Everly," I whisper, but she doesn't look up.

Her eyes are closed and her mouth moves quickly. She's chanting something, but the words are impossible to decipher.

"Everly," I say louder, but she either doesn't hear me or ignores me. Either way, she continues her chanting.

I dare to step into the circle and the point at which I do, her eyes fly open, and anger fills their depths.

"What are you doing? You should know better than to step into a dryad's circle," she says, clearly miffed.

"I'm here to make sure you're okay," I tell her, figuring that part should be obvious. Our understanding has been in place for long enough now.

She scoffs and turns her attention back to her joined hands. She breathes deeply and closes her eyes. "I'm fine. I don't need all of you constantly fawning over me," she says. "I need to be left alone."

"And why is that?" I ask, frustrated because being left along is exactly what she *doesn't* need. I crease my brow and turn the rest of the way to face her, folding my arms across my chest.

"Because I'm frustrated!" she rails at me.

"Why are you frustrated?"

She inhales deeply. "Because Harlow tried to make me remember at least something about him and *us*, but that didn't work, so I asked Jean-Claude to bite me, thinking it might remind me of something about him and Dread and all of you, but *that* didn't work either."

I feel like telling her I know there was more that went on between her and the count, but I don't. I hold back and try to keep my own jealousy under control. It's really none of my business what she does with anyone, even if the truth does burn like all the fires of hell.

"So now I'm here, in the woods, trying to do something that reminds me of home, but even that is failing. Nothing is working." Once she's finished firing off like a machine gun, she takes a settling breath.

I lock eyes with her and she sighs, shaking her head. She holds my gaze and her eyes go soft, filling with unshed tears. I can see how much this whole situation bothers her. It's eating at her and I can't even begin to imagine what she's going through.

"I'm sorry," she says. "I didn't mean to snap at you. I'm just frustrated."

"I get it."

"I was trying to create a circle, but I can't even do that right!"

"It's okay," I say calmly. "You'll get your memories back."

"You don't know that."

I'm surprised by her lack of optimism because it goes against everything I know of her as a dryad. Post-purge Everly is different though, darker around the edges somehow. It's like that innocence that used to characterize her isn't there anymore—strangely, she seems older now, wiser, more experienced. Different. But still, she's every bit as lovely as the first time I saw her in class at Ever Dark.

"I *do* know you'll get your memories back eventually," I say. "You're stronger than you know. If you set your mind to it, you'll achieve whatever you want to. I have no doubt."

She scoffs. "Well, that makes one of us, then."

"Keep strong and have faith that your memories will come back to you in their own time." I offer her a smile, but I can tell by her expression that she doesn't believe me. And it's not enough that I believe me. Or, at least, I believe Riven when he says her memories will return. "Believe what Riven says, Everly."

"Why?" she fires back. "Riven means nothing to me."

"Because he knows what he's talking about. He hasn't steered us wrong yet."

A strange mix of emotions appears on her face. A flicker of surprise, curiosity, suspicion, and finally, acceptance. She nods once and looks to the ground. It's a few long seconds before she meets my eyes again.

"Thank you," she says.

"For what?"

"For not being frustrated or sad or disappointed with me," she answers. "I just... it's hard on me—all of this. The not remembering, not knowing who to trust, not being sure what to believe. And it makes it even harder when Jean-Claude and Harlow seem so upset or irritated or sad... I don't know what the best word is... It's hard on me because I can tell I'm hurting them, and I'm not even doing anything..."

"It's not your fault, and you're doing the best you can." I take a breath. "And if they can't accept that, that's on them, not you."

She nods and gives me an appreciative smile. "It's nice to be around someone who doesn't look at me like I'm something to fix."

I chuckle lightly.

"What's funny?" she asks.

"You hardly need fixing, Everly."

"You aren't annoyed that I don't remember you?"

I shrug. "You remember what you remember. I believe connections like ours always come back—they just need time. *You* need time. I'm not worried about it."

"You sound confident."

"I am."

She nods, but I can see there's more in her eyes—something that doesn't add up, something that's still bothering her.

"What is it?" I ask.

"It's just... I don't know who I'm meant to be loyal to..."

"I don't know what you mean," I say honestly.

She sighs and looks off to the side. "Well, Harlow and Jean-Claude... they both make it seem like we had *histories* and I feel something for each of them. Feelings I don't really understand, but they're there, all the same. It's like I had something with each of them, something beyond just friendship—"

"You did and you still do," I finish for her.

She frowns up at me. "Do we have something between us too?" she asks me. "You and I?"

"I'm your friend," I answer, but I can't help the fact that my tone of voice drops because the truth of the matter is that even though she and I were only ever friends, I always wanted to be more with her. "And if I can give you a word of advice?"

"Yes."

"The present is the only time in which we have any real power. The past and future aren't now— what's done is done and what's coming will come, you know?"

Everly is quiet for a moment.

"We were good friends, weren't we?" she asks shyly.

I nod again.

She crosses her arms and leans back against a tree and then slides down the bark and plops on the ground, her lavender hair bunching on top of her head. I go to sit beside her, and she gives me an encouraging smile. I pull her gently to me, letting her rest against my body as I lean against the tree.

"Will you tell me about us?" she asks.

"Us?"

She nods. "From the moment we met each other. Will you tell me where we were and how we became friends? Anything you can remember at all."

I nod as I reach down and clear a stray tendril of hair from her face. Then I tell her about how our friendship began, when she first walked into my class at Ever Dark Academy and how I was taken with her from that very moment.

I don't know how long it is that we talk and laugh and reminisce and even though Everly doesn't remember anything I'm telling her, I know my words are reassuring—or, at least, she says they are.

It might be an hour later or two when Riddle appears in the air, carrying Dorian's journal, as if reminding Everly what she *should* be doing. And reminiscing with me isn't it.

He circles around us a few times before dropping the journal. I catch it midair and hand it to Everly as Riddle lands on the ground before hobbling to his owner and settling in her lap. She scratches his head and he chirps at her. Turning to face the book, she sighs.

"I guess there's no time like the present," she says while opening the leather cover.

"I'm also curious to see what it says."

She nods and glancing down, I notice the pages are empty. Blank. She pages through a few more of them and it's the same—nothing.

"It's empty," I say, unable to hide my shock.

"No," she answers as she shakes her head. "It's not empty to me."

"You can see something?" I ask, frowning because the pages are nothing but white as I look down at them.

"Yes," she answers, but there's a look of confusion in her eyes.

"You can see words?"

"Not words," she answers and shakes her head. "There are a bunch of images or... glyphs...

shapes that I can't understand. It's like it's written in another language."

"Yet you were able to read it before."

She looks over at me with wide eyes. "I don't remember how I was able to."

With that, Riddle leans over the book and opening his beak, releases what sounds like a burp accompanied with a flame of fire that lights up the book and, suddenly, I can see the glyphs she's talking about—they appear all over the pages, lit up in orange as if reflecting a setting sun. A second later, though, there's nothing there again.

"They disappeared again," I say.

Everly looks down at the book and nods, then shakes her head. "All I can see are the same glyphs I saw before, but I can't make sense of them."

She looks up at me then, concern and confusion in her beautiful eyes.

"What do you think that means?" I ask.

"I don't know."

EIGHT
♀♥♂♂♂♂
Everly

I sense the light in my dream a second before I wake.

A dryad's first call to nature is always the sunrise. I feel it like a vibration in my bones, my own vitality rising up to meet the sky.

My eyes open, and I stare out the window. There's a thicket of ivy winding down the side of the castle just outside my sill. I can see the top of it from where I lie on the bed.

Last I remember, I was lying under a tree in Griim's lap in the forest of Castle Raven Night as he told me our history.

I yawn and rotate my neck only to catch sight of Griim's sleeping face, where he's propped against one of the pillows beside me. It takes me a moment or two to remember the evening before—how we talked for hours and then walked back to my bedroom. How I begged him to stay with me when he said he should be going. How, all the while, memories of Jean-Claude touching me, biting me, filled my head, and I wasn't sure what to do with them. Not that I'm sure what to do with them now.

Of all of them, I feel the most comfortable with Griim, even after everything that passed between Jean-Claude and me. Actually, maybe that's the reason I'm nervous about the vampire. I just... feel something for him. Something I don't want to explore. And I also feel something for Harlow that's equally hard to define.

Yet, I can define what I feel for Griim—*trust*. I feel like I can trust him, like he's a true friend to me. There's just an easy affability between us and he's the least... intimidating. He's handsome definitely, but not in the steely and intense way Jean-Claude is handsome. And he doesn't have that bad-boy, give-no-fucks attitude of Harlow. Griim's attractiveness is more approachable. The feelings I have towards him are those of a friend and maybe that's why I'm so much more comfortable around him. With Harlow and Jean-Claude, I know there was something more between us because I can feel as much, even if I don't possess the memories to accompany the feelings.

As I look at Griim and remember how easy it was to talk with him and laugh with him last night, I find myself smiling. I can't help but trace a line down his temple from his forehead down to the bowing shape of his lips. At my touch, his eyes drift open.

"Good morning," I say, smiling. "How'd you sleep?"

"Like a baby," he answers. "How did you sleep?"

"Fine," I tell him honestly. "Surprisingly fine, given everything that's happened and given the fact that there's a war soon to be looming over us."

"Unless Riven can talk his way out of it."

I nod. "Right and... what are the chances of that?"

He shrugs. "I don't know... Riven is pretty persuasive." He reaches over and brushes a few strands of hair off my exposed shoulder.

"You know, I've never understood that phrase," I tell him, going back to our first topic of conversation.

"What phrase?"

"Saying you slept 'like a baby' to mean you slept *well*," I answer on a shrug. "I mean, have you ever been around a baby? They sleep for twenty minutes at a time and constantly wake up crying."

Griim laughs. "You have a point," he says. "Next time I'll say I slept like a rock. It's more accurate, anyway." He points to himself with his free thumb. "Made of clay, after all."

"Hmm." I smile at him. "That's hard to believe sometimes... that you aren't..."

"Real?" he offers.

"Flesh," I answer, shaking my head. "And *you are real*."

Riddle suddenly appears above us, swirling around the air before he drops down and lands on the ground with a plopping sort of sound. Then he extends his neck and chirps. I reach down and pet his feathered head, and he makes a purring sound at me.

"He's a good little... Riddle," Griim says as he looks at my familiar and smiles.

I nod, facing Griim while he stands up and reaches down, offering both his hands to me. Taking them, he helps me up to a sitting position. His eyes are locked on mine now. We both remain like that for a few seconds before he glances down at his wristwatch. All of a sudden, his hands slip free of mine and he turns to leave.

"Where are you going?" I ask.

"It's almost nine," he announces. "I have to be at Ever Dark in fifteen minutes for my first training session with the Elementals."

"Already?"

He nods and immediately crosses over to the fireplace, where he leans down and looks at the deeply singed wood (which is nothing more than charcoal really) in the hearth. He breathes on the barely-there flames and they respond as if he'd just dumped kerosene on them. I know Griim travels through fire and I figure that's what he's about to do. Before he does, though, he turns to face me.

"Thanks," he says.

"For what?"

"Just for being a good friend," he says. "For a minute there, I wasn't sure I'd ever get you back."

He smiles, then turns to the fireplace and takes a step forward, his toes touching the flames.

"Griim!"

He turns around to face me again, brow creased curiously.

"Take me with you," I say. "I don't want to be stuck in here all day, bored out of my mind."

"You're supposed to be reading Dorian's book."

"Right, and I can still read while I watch you train." I can't quite explain it, but being near him brings me a tranquility I haven't known since I lost my memories. "Please?"

"You're supposed to stay here," he argues. "Harlow's supposed to have watch today and Harlow's a serious pain in the ass when he's angry—more so than normal."

"Last I saw Harlow, he left me to my own defenses and wasn't exactly very friendly about it. I'd rather you take me to watch you train and you can keep an eye on me there… while I read."

Something flashes in his golden eyes, and his smile widens an almost indiscernible amount. He extends a hand, and I take it.

"Looks like we're going the long way, then."

He doesn't sound disappointed.

Watching Griim train is magical.

And his magic is different from anything I've ever seen before. Like all things enchanting, Griim's power is an extension of his most authentic self, but it's so much more than that. It's nothing at all like the magic of dryads. Until I came here, I thought my mother was the most powerful creature on the goddess's green earth. The things I saw her do in my youth still boggle my mind.

As much as I love my mother, appreciate her grace, her elegance, her stern compassion and her unceasing fortitude, there has always been a level of tension between us. She's always expected me to become High Priestess of the Circle. There was never any doubt in her mind that I would be the next of the goddess's chosen ones. And that was a lot of responsibility and pressure to put on me. Only, before I never realized it. Now I do.

Now I'm not sure if I want the same thing for myself—to become High Priestess. Before, there was never a question about it—I just blindly accepted whatever my mother wanted. What she wanted was what I wanted, too. But now? Now I'm not so sure...

Of course, Mother doesn't know about any of this—any of what happened from the moment my train got stuck in Dread. And, strangely enough, I haven't wanted to tell her. I haven't even *tried* to tell her—instead, I've just allowed her to think I've been in Arcadia all this time, studying at the Academy of Enchantment... a place I absolutely detest.

But back to the Elementals training in front of me... each requires their own particular element in order to call their magic. Hence, the water elementals travel with hydration packs of water or ice, and the fire elementals rely on matches or lighters to provide them with a flame (if they're being lazy—usually they can summon up a flame all on their own). For the elementals that bend earth and air, their materials are all around them. The coalition of all four elementals together is more magnificent than a rainbow over a pot of genuine leprechaun's gold.

Dryad magic is powerful, to be sure, but it's lighter than elemental magic, hollower. While Dryad magic could be compared to a soap bubble, elemental magic is like the fire from a dragon. Strong and gritty and powerful as hell.

"Alright," Griim shouts to the army of at least fifty elementals. "Run that last drill again. Maeve, I wanna see some real speed from you, and Hector, let yourself off the goddamned leash. You're only using half your potential."

Two of his students nod.

At Griim's command, the entirety of the flat, green field erupts into a flurry of fire, water, violent wind, and crushing earth. It feels like watching the world combust inwardly on itself—like an earthquake, followed by a tsunami and then a firestorm. Absolutely mind-boggling.

The training fields at Ever Dark Academy are vast and largely unkempt. There are infinite patches of weeds that hang low to the ground. And the fencing around the area is shoddy and made mostly of broken barbed wire. It used to be a place where students would trade illicit potions, potions which Riven very cleverly reappropriated for the coming war.

War.

That thought makes me go cold.

War is such a foreign concept to me as a dryad, like something out of an old, dark fairy tale. We don't trade in violence. We don't fight in wars. And we certainly don't fight them in Dread.

Oh, goddess, what will Mother say when she hears about this?

I promptly shake that thought out of my head. There's no use dwelling over things I can't change. And I won't be able to talk to her, not until I'm back home. And I won't be able to return home for a long time—not with the borders being the way they are. Strangely enough, I can't say I'm that bothered by that realization. And, given the option, I wouldn't return home. I'd stay right where I am.

Somewhere in the middle of the attack drill, Griim whips off his long-sleeved T-shirt to reveal a shockingly toned stomach and muscular arms. They were so much less obvious under the shirt. He wipes sweat from his brow and runs a hand through his shaggy gray hair. We lock eyes for the briefest of seconds, and I feel my heart jump in my chest.

Jeez, what is with me lately? I think to myself. *First, Harlow gets me all riled up and then that whole situation with Jean-Claude happened—a situation I still can't get out of my mind. And now watching Griim training is turning me on?*

My pulse quickens.

My face flushes.

My hands get sweaty in the palms.

My knees even start to go a bit wobbly. It's barely noticeable, any of it, very subtle physiological changes, but I catch each and every one as it happens. It's a bit like what Harlow forced me to feel only natural, subtle and slow rather than a burning blaze. Still, the feelings build, and I can't tear my eyes away from Griim.

The smooth long lines of muscle move so elegantly. And with such speed! He's like a gazelle, but somehow, he's also the lion pursuing the gazelle. Strength and tenacity held in a cage.

"Take ten!" Griim yells.

He jogs over to where I sit at the base of a tall tree.

"You bored out of your wits yet?" Griim asks as Riddle chirps a greeting from the lowest branch of the tree above me.

"Are you joking?" I laugh and shake my head. "That was some of the most spell-binding tactical magic I've ever seen! Griim it's... you're... all of it's just incredible!"

He chuckles low in his chest, a rumbling sound.

"Thanks," he says. "A few more weeks and we'll all be back in fighting shape. It'll come easier after that."

Even as he says the words, I wonder if we have a few more weeks before this battle ensues. Suddenly, the smile washes off Griim's face and his expression turns sober, and his usual air of intensity returns to him. I can tell there's something pressing on his mind.

"What's wrong?"

He swallows hard, as if he isn't sure if he should tell me or not. "I have a meeting with Riven tonight."

"Really?" I ask, eyebrows raised.

"Really."

"Did he say what it's about?"

"No, but I'm assuming it's general battle strategy." He drops to his knees, sitting beside me on the blanket. "I figure he wants an update on how the army's fairing and maybe he wants to give us an update on his attempted peace talks with Granger."

I nod thoughtfully.

"And how *is* the army fairing?" I ask shyly, not wanting to intrude but desperately wanting to know.

"Worried for your safety, Miss Stillwater?" he asks in a mock serious tone as he gives me an elevated eyebrow of amusement.

"I'm just... wondering when the fighting will start?"

"Who knows?" Griim shakes his head and lets out an elongated breath. "It could be a week, a month, maybe more. As with all things between the academies, there is protocol..."

"Even in war?"

"Even in war," he affirms. "But don't worry. I trust Riven and whatever happens, we'll be ready."

"I don't doubt it," I say. "But I can't really help but worry."

"You're a dryad," he says with a grin. "It's in your nature to care about the well-being of others.

It's a good trait to have. Don't fault yourself for it."

He chuckles, but it does nothing to placate my fears.

"I just... I'm worried for you. For all of you."

"Everly," Griim reaches for my hands and, taking them, brings them to his mouth and kisses each of them, an intensely ponderous look on his face. "I'm not just a fire elemental, you know?"

"You're not?"

"No." He shakes his head. "I'm not."

"You're also... a Gemini?" I ask, attempting to make a joke, but it doesn't really land right.

"I'm also Cackus's familiar."

I squint and tilt my head to the side, giving him a curious look. "You're his familiar?" I ask in bewilderment. "How does that work exactly? I mean, Cackus is a dragon and, hence, you're a dragon's familiar—I get that, but... what does that mean?"

"You are full of questions," Griim says, smiling. "You know that?"

"I do," I say. "It's an incurable affliction, I'm afraid."

"Well, my being a familiar to Cackus is a bit like you and Riddle but on a bigger scale," he says simply. "Cackus forged me the way you forged

Riddle and he filled me with his fire like I filled Riddle with mine."

"Does that mean he can't be killed?" I hope the answer is yes.

"He can be killed, but it's a very difficult thing to kill a dragon."

"Oh," I answer.

"And as long as Cackus is alive, so am I," Griim continues. "He can respawn me if I'm destroyed, but I don't *die* unless Cackus does."

"But Cackus isn't fighting in the battle with you?" I ask, hope in my voice.

He shakes his head regretfully. "He is."

I let out a little moan of anguish at that. And then I wonder if my reaction is silly because a dragon in battle is probably pretty much untouchable. If anything, having Cackus by their side should be a good thing, not a bad thing.

"Don't worry," Griim says, laughing sweetly and stroking my hair. "Cackus is one of the most skilled fighters I've ever known—"

"And a big target," I counter.

"Fair enough," he says. "But the old geezer's been around for hundreds of years. I don't see something as dumb as a silly border dispute sending him to his eternal rest."

It's really not a border dispute between the two academies, but I don't say as much. Everyone already knows it. "Shouldn't Cackus be training with you?"

"Cackus is like our secret weapon against the Academy of Enchantment," he says, something like a proud gleam in his eye. "He doesn't need to train. He just needs to show up."

I sigh heavily, letting my eyes close. "If you say so."

"I do," he says, then sighs himself. "I have to get back to training."

I feel the soft pressure of his lips against my forehead and then a hesitancy. His breath hitches. It's like he's catching himself in the act, and I open my eyes to give him a little reassuring smile. The relief in his eyes sends a wave of happiness through me.

"I have to go," he whispers.

"I know." I look up at him, staring into his golden eyes, getting a bit lost.

And then Griim is up and off to the training grounds again.

NINE
♀♥♂♂♂♂
Griim

The last twenty-four hours have me in a goddamn fit, and I don't use that word lightly.

I'm exhausted after hours of training, completely sapped of my life force. But still, I feel completely awake, simply because Everly is holding my hand and resting her head on my shoulder. War with Arcadia and the Academy of Enchantment is most probably coming, but for now, life couldn't be better.

"What time is it?" she asks as the moonlight streams over her face, highlighting her beauty.

"I think it's almost eleven," I answer with a quick glance back at the open front door of Castle Raven Night. The two of us have just walked in from the training grounds.

"How did the reading go?" I ask.

She shakes her head and then sighs. "It didn't. I couldn't make sense of anything in the book."

"Same as before?"

She nods. "Same as before. Just all these strange glyphs." She breathes out a frustrated sigh. "I wonder if I was ever really able to read it at all. Maybe all this fuss over me having read Dorian's journal is for nothing."

"I don't think that's the case."

She looks up at me. "What do you think is the case then?"

I shrug. "Who knows? Maybe the book is just waiting for the right time to reveal itself to you again?" I pause. "I mean, it revealed itself to you before so why wouldn't it do the same now?"

"I don't know," she answers and then sighs again, letting her head fall back as she does. "It's just another thing that doesn't make any damned sense," she says, surprising me to hear her swear. In general, dryads don't swear—at least that's what Everly had told me when she'd first arrived here. But, apparently those same rules no longer apply to her.

Yes, she's definitely different—not so innocent. I don't think that's a bad thing though.

"Need me to tuck you in?" I ask, trying to keep any trace of hope from my voice, but I have a sinking feeling I'm unsuccessful. "I've gotten excellent reviews."

"I'm good," she says as she looks up at me and gives me a pat on my arm. "Go to your meeting with Riven. I wouldn't want you to keep him waiting—I'm sure it's important and... I'm going to give Dorian's book another try."

"Okay," I say. "Goodnight, Everly."

She answers in kind as I brush my lips lightly against her temple and shut the door behind her.

"Griim!" Harlow's voice booms up at me from the base of the stairs. He takes the steps two at a time, leather jacket clearly bunched up his ass.

"What?" I ask, despite being patently uninterested.

"Where the hell have you been?"

I walk past him, down the stairs and into the foyer, and Harlow has no choice but to follow if he wants to keep having a conniption with me as witness. So, we descend the stairs, and I continue to ignore him. Mainly because I know it will piss him off.

"Griim!"

I stop walking just shy of the door and turn to face him. "What?"

"You heard me ask you a question," he says. His curly brown hair is matted against his forehead with sweat. He's breathing heavily, and his leather jacket is dusty so I figure he's been flying. Probably for what must have been a long time—if his overall sweaty disposition is any sign.

"What do you want?" I ask.

"*Where were you today?*"

"I was training. Where the hell do you think I was?"

"And you didn't think to mention you were taking Everly with you? Nevermind that you also ignored the fact that it was my shift?"

I give Harlow an incredulous look. "Since when is it your style to sound like a hall monitor? Everly was with me. She was safe, and frankly, she's not too eager to spend more time with you after—"

"What?" Harlow squints and gets in my face, only a few inches from me and almost my same height. "What did she tell you? Did she remember something?"

"No, she doesn't remember anything other than you being an asshole about her memory loss."

"Hmph." Harlow's expression is disbelieving. "So explain something to me."

"What?"

"Why is she all buddy-buddy with you when Count Dick and I are obviously still strangers to her. What's the damn difference?"

Little does he know Count Dick isn't exactly a stranger to her anymore—something I'm not about to mention because Harlow is already pissed off and I'm really not in the mood to see his impersonation of a volcano.

I hesitate with how to answer. "If she's buddy-buddy with me, it's because I'm not trying to make her into anything other than what she is."

"What the hell are you talking about?"

I glare at him. "I'm talking about the fact that I've accepted her memory loss. I've accepted the fact that she can't remember me and... you haven't."

He rolls his eyes and throws his hands up in mock applause. "Oh, the noble and sensitive Griim. You want an award or what?"

"This isn't a game, Harlow."

"Says the man in the lead." Harlow crosses his arms and takes a step back. "You know the most frustrating part about this whole shit show is that if Everly had even a fraction of her memories, she'd be spending all her time with me—just like she used to."

"You don't know that."

"I *do* know that."

I shake my head. "Maybe you want to believe it, but Everly chose to spend her day with me today simply because I make her feel safe. Maybe you should start thinking about how your actions are affecting her and not just what she can do for you."

"You don't understand how goddamn frustrating it is to watch her not remember—"

"Are you shitting me?" I ask him, narrowing my eyes at him as I shake my head. "Of course, I do!"

If Harlow thinks he can saunter in here in that stupid leather jacket and lecture me about Everly, he's got another think coming. His selfish incubus ways are getting on my last nerve, and elementals have always been known for our legendary tempers, along with our legendary self-control. But, at this moment, I'm feeling one a little stronger than the other.

"I've been praying to gods and goddesses I don't even believe in that Everly will get her memories back," I surge on, trying to stifle the need to sucker punch him. But I'm no fool—Harlow might be a dumbass but he's also a strong and powerful dumbass. "I'm more frustrated than I've ever been in my goddamned life," I continue. "I've been killing myself trying not to pressure her or goad her or make her feel broken, and here you are with all your horny agendas making her feel like a huge disappointment because you can't magically undo a purge put into place by a skilled sorcerer!" I run my hands through my hair and take a step toward him when I notice he's silent for once. "And another thing," I continue. "Everly is my friend before she's anything else. And that means I'm going to protect her. Even from you."

"She doesn't need to be protected from me," he says finally.

"Regardless, she came to me because she wanted me to keep an eye on her, not you. She trusts me, not you. And I know you fucking hate that but it remains the truth."

"What a load of shit!" Harlow bursts out. He might be a little drunk by the look and smell of him. He's managed not to slur his speech so far, but he's starting to slip. "You're so fucking high and mighty up there on your white horse. Must be a good feeling to be the unthreatening little puppy dog that makes Everly feel right at home."

"Whatever—I'm done with this conversation." I start to walk away but his grip around my upper arm stops me.

"Let me tell you something, fire-breath," he continues, putting his finger right in my face. "You may be her security blanket right now, but when her memories come back, and they *will* come back, she's going to remember that you don't mean jack shit to her. She's going to remember that you're nothing but the familiar to the Academy's pet dragon. She's going to remember how pathetic you really are. And most importantly, she's going to remember *me*."

I laugh. With my whole chest. "You really shouldn't be fighting in this battle at all," I nearly spit the words at him.

"And why is that?"

I glare at him. "Because there's no point in you risking your life for a girl you clearly don't understand."

"I understand her," Harlow shoots back, shaking his head. "We understand each other."

"No, you don't. You don't even know her."

A flash of rage appears in his dark brown eyes. "You fucking take that back."

"I haven't said anything that isn't the truth," I say, shaking my head. "The same can't be said for you."

"I know her better than—"

"Harlow, listen to what you're saying," I say, my volume rising. "You're treating this like it's some moronic competition for Everly's attention. All of your swagger and bullshit doesn't fucking matter right now. So, check that jealousy shit at the door because none of us have time for your insecurities."

To my surprise, he's quiet for a second. His face is still stuck in that smug, cocky, smirk, but it's faded slightly, twitched down at the corners. I'm not sure how much time passes—seconds or maybe minutes.

Suddenly, Harlow pulls his arm back and takes a swing at me. I dodge the blow, but just barely. At the exact moment that his fist sails past my face, I summon a flame in my hand and hold it right in front of his eyes.

"Careful," I say.

His body is tense, ready to pounce. But slowly he relaxes. I take a deep breath and watch as he loosens his arms and hands.

"Look, this isn't a game to me either," he says as he leans back against the stone wall of Castle Raven Night. "I just... I *need* her to remember. You don't understand how badly I need her to remember."

"I know you do," I say plainly, allowing the flame to die in my palm. "But you need to think about what *she* needs right now. We all do." And on that topic, there's one more subject I want to address with him. "And I'm going to suppose you're keeping your brother away from her?"

"Why is everyone so concerned about Lennox?" he demands.

"Um, have you met him?"

"Obviously." He shakes his head and further glares at me. "I can handle my brother."

"Riven didn't seem to think so."

Harlow faces me with narrowed eyes. "The last thing I'm going to do is introduce Everly to Lennox when she can't even remember me. Not only that, but she doesn't trust me which means she wouldn't trust me if I warned her against Lennox."

I hold up my hands. "Hey, all I'm saying is just keep him away from her."

"And that's exactly what I'm doing."

"Is Lennox training with you? Did you recruit him with the rest of the demons?"

Harlow frowns at me. "What do you think?" When I don't answer, he continues. "Riven's instructions were for me to assemble *all* the demons. Well, 'all' includes my brother."

"Keep him away from her," I repeat.

"No need to tell me, fire-boy. I was already making sure Lennox is as far from Everly as far is possible to be."

TEN
♀♥♂♂♂♂
Everly

After Griim leaves my room, I turn to face Riddle, where he sits on his perch by my bed. Dorian's book is lying on my comforter and the worn leather face seems to be calling to me.

"I don't know what the point of trying again is," I mutter beneath my breath as I approach the bed and, sitting down, lift the book into my lap, angst stirring deep within my stomach. "It's not like I can understand the damn thing."

Riddle flaps his wings above me and I take that as a sign that I should give it another try. I breathe in deeply and look up at him with a smile.

"Caw, caw," he calls back.

"Here goes," I say as I reach down to open the front cover, but before I can even touch the worn binding, the cover blows open and thumps my thigh hard enough to sting. Then it's as though all the winds of the forest are gathered within the book because they suddenly come shooting out and blast me right in the face. I close my eyes against the bluster as I hear the pages turning in swift succession, one after the other.

"What the hell?" I start as Riddle chirps above me, sounding like he's as startled as I am. All I can think of doing is closing the book so I can stop the wind attack, but before I'm able to touch the leather, the winds stop blowing and the pages stop turning. The book just lies there, completely dormant. Then it flips a page, then two, then three.

"Oh, no, you don't," I start as I try to close it, but I have to wrestle with it—it refuses to close! I drop it back into my lap and it quickly opens to what appears to be the dead center of the journal and then... nothing. No wind. No psychotic pages turning. The book just lays there like it didn't just completely freak out.

As I glance down at it, strange symbols surge forth again, covering the blank pages with bizarre letters and numbers that don't belong to any alphabet I've ever seen. They flit across the pages, some of them highlighted in metallic gold and silver. Others are just plain black. As I watch the shapes drift in and out of the pages, some of the letters begin to stay longer than the others. It's almost as if the pages are sticky and cling to a few of the letters.

"Y.O.U.R," I repeat as the letters appear in large, blocky script at the top of the page. "M.E.," I continue spelling the letters out as they appear. "*Memories*."

Riddle squawks at me and I nod, but don't tear my attention away from the book.

"My memories what?"

As I watch the pages laid out before me, more and more letters and numbers of all different sizes continue to bleed in and out of the parchment, until an "A" remains. Then an "R" which is followed by an "E."

"*Your memories are,*" I read out as my heart starts pounding in my chest and I wonder what in the nine hells the book knows about my missing memories. What is it trying to tell me?

"R," I call out and Riddle flies around my head, clearly as excited as I am. "E!"

By the time the final letter of the word arrives, I call out: "*Your memories are returned!*"

As soon as the words leave my mouth, something strange happens. It's like everything around me begins to dissolve into drips of color— as though watching a freshly painted work of art doused in water. The droplets run down the canvas and the colors mix together until they're nothing but various shades of gray.

"Riddle?" I say as I continue to watch the room dissolve into mundane gray. As I turn to my familiar, I realize he's the same colors he always is and when I glance down at myself, the case is the same with me. I haven't changed. Neither has Riddle. Yet everything around me is...

"What the hell?" I ask as I turn around and around again, trying to make sense of the fact that everything is colorful again—as if the dripping oil painting was set to rewind and all the paint had been returned to its proper location.

I blink and then blink again.

What in the heck is going on?

My head suddenly feels... full again. Complete. No longer missing... everything.

"Castle Raven Night," I whisper as I glance around myself and take in the unicorns and the hearts all over my bed and curtains. I turn around and recognize the armoire with the weird dolls and the white desk. I face the bed again and I've never been happier to see the boy band posters. But this time, instead of considering them with an odd sense of detachment, I look at my surroundings with appreciation because I remember Stregen picked everything out for me before I ever moved here.

Stregen... Jean-Claude's loyal servant.

Jean-Claude…

"I remember!" I yell out, ecstatic. "Riddle! I remember!"

Riddle flaps around my head, as if flying on his own happiness at my outburst. My memories have been returned to me and that has everything to do with the book, with Dorian's journal. I don't understand how or why, but I'm jubilantly excited, all the same.

As I look at Dorian's journal and reach for it, I'm suddenly overwhelmed with memories of the book—of a faun named Kinsey, who directed me to the book in the library at the Academy of Enchantment. I remember how Professor Ingram demanded to know if I was able to read it. I remember… I remember Dorian's entries—well, at least the ones I read. And I remember what happened to me at their hands—the centaurs, Professor Ingram—the purging… I remember all of it.

Grabbing the book again and eager for what more I can learn, I race through the pages, but frown as soon as I realize they're all blank. Every single one of them is void of anything—no glyphs, no images, no symbols, no letters or numbers. There's nothing.

"I don't understand," I say in a hollow voice as I shake my head. "Why won't you reveal yourself to me?"

I want to scream, want to throw the book across the room or tear out the pages, but I do nothing. I just stare down at the journal as I try to understand why it's hiding from me.

Riddle continues to flap overhead and I'm sure he can feel the frustration and confusion flowing through me. But there's also an overwhelming surge of complete and total happiness over the fact that the men of Dread are now no longer strangers to me.

"Everly?"

I turn to my door at the sound of Jean-Claude's voice.

"Are you well?" he asks, frowning at me because he clearly doesn't understand what's going on and, no doubt, heard all the ruckus Riddle and I have been making.

"I'm more than well," I answer as I hop off the bed and hurry towards him as his eyes widen. When I reach him, I pause for a moment or two as memories of the old Jean-Claude battle with the memories we've most recently made—*sexual* memories. Before he can say another word, I lean up on my tip-toes and throw my arms around him.

"I can remember, Jean-Claude," I whisper. "I can remember… everything."

"Our resident oracle has had a vision," Riven says as we gather around him in his office, an hour or so after I explained to Jean-Claude that somehow, some way, Dorian's journal returned my memories to me.

Of course, everyone was elated to learn as much, no one more so than Harlow. But once that conversation was exhausted, Riven cleared his throat and turned the subject to more pressing concerns.

And now as we all look at him, his expression is stern, his lips a hard line. "According to the vision, the Academy of Enchantment's army are already enroute."

"They're already enroute?" I repeat as my mouth drops open. "But… it hasn't… it hasn't even been a week! I thought there was protocol they had to follow? I thought there was red tape they had to get through?" No one says anything, but the outrage within me doesn't subside. Outrage and confusion. "You said this would take a while!

You said it wasn't something that would happen right away!"

Riven turns to look at me and shakes his head, rubbing the back of his neck. "It is what it is."

"But what about the formality of announcing an invasion?" I continue, trying to shake the sense of shock that's already overtaken me. I just don't understand how our enemies are already on their way to us. They've broken the protocol, and no one seems to be addressing that.

Riven inhales deeply. "I believe Granger has it in his mind that because we breached border protocol, he's not interested in war formalities."

I swallow hard.

"Then it's war?" Griim asks.

Riven turns to the fire elemental and nods. "That means we have mere days to prepare, and that's why I gathered you all here—to tell you to get your brigades in order."

"We need to get Everly somewhere safe—" Harlow says as he turns to look at me.

"I don't want to be sequestered away during the fighting," I say, shaking my head. "I want to fight alongside all of you." I take a deep breath. "You know you can use my magic. It's strong and stronger than most anyone in your army."

There's a brief and charged moment of utter silence.

"Everly, the whole reason for this battle is you," Riven answers in a subdued yet stern tone. "If you're fighting and someone from their side spots you, they'll either kill you on the spot or take you with them." He frowns at me and I can tell his words are hard on him. As a shadow demon, he feels everything so much more than the rest of us. "It's too dangerous."

"Um," Griim starts, but Harlow interrupts.

"Are you out of your mind?" he asks and stares at me with an angry look. "You could get killed."

"So could you," I answer, narrowing my eyes at him—Harlow has been difficult lately from what I can remember of most recent events. Not that that's really such a surprise—Harlow has always been difficult. But now I'm determined and he's about to see how difficult I can be. They all are.

"Don't be dumb, Everly," Harlow says.

Since my argument won't be settled by Harlow—only by Riven—I return my attention to him. "I have training," I continue. "My magic is incredibly strong. I've now trained at three academies."

"I'm aware," Riven says and nods, but doesn't appear in the least bit convinced. "But I'm not willing to risk you."

"None of us are," Jean-Claude adds.

I look at him and shake my head. "I'm a gifted student, and I'm good with defensive *and* offensive magic," I insist as I then stand up and Riddle swirls around my head, cawing and chirping at anyone who will listen. I'm not sure what he's trying to say, if anything at all. "I can hold my own, and I can be useful in a battle." I pause to look at each of them in turn, wanting them to understand how serious I am. We are all in this together and I don't want to be hidden away while they risk their lives... for me. "And... it would be easy for me to disguise myself with magic."

The light from the candle on Riven's desk dances against the black leather of Harlow's jacket as he walks from Riven's desk to stand a foot in front of me. His eyes are narrowed and his jaw is tight. I already know where he stands on this subject and I'm not interested in what more he wants to say.

"No," Harlow says in a voice that brooks no arguments. "We can't risk it."

"Yet you can risk yourselves?" I demand, angry.

He nods. "This whole battle is about keeping you safe."

I lift my eyebrows, look Harlow up and down, and cross my arms over my chest. He turns the full brunt of his angry gaze on me, but I don't shrink under the scrutiny.

"She's not fighting," Harlow says, turning his gaze from me to the others in the room.

"You don't speak for her," Griim responds.

"Maybe I should!" Harlow yells back at him, shaking his head as he throws his arms up into the air. Out of all of them, Harlow is the most dramatic. "I'm the only one making any goddamn sense!"

"Enough." Riven lifts a silencing finger.

I notice with interest that Jean-Claude doesn't say anything which isn't like him. I can only wonder why. Regardless, a hush falls over the room.

Riven levels me with a stern expression. Then he breathes in deeply. "You can't fight."

My heart breaks with anger as I shake my head and take a step closer. "But Riven—"

"I'm sorry," he says and shakes his head. He's clearly made up his mind and, as with most things, his word is final. "But Harlow is right in certain respects. Our priority is keeping you protected…"

"I could be useful," I insist, tears starting to sting my eyes. "I'm a powerful dryad—"

"I know you are," Riven says, placing a hand gingerly on my shoulder. As soon as he touches me, I can feel all the worry and dread filling him and I want to do everything I can to help him, to make him understand that more able bodies are better than fewer.

"Far too powerful a dryad to risk on the battlefield and... there's still Dorian's journal," Riven continues. "We still have to uncover what's so important about it. You're the only one who can read and understand it, Everly."

"The pages are blank!" I insist.

Riven shakes his head. "I have a feeling they won't always be. The book restored your memories—it's not just going to leave you in the lurch now. There's more to be learned, and you're the only one who has access to the knowledge within it."

He turns to the room at large. "Ready your armies," he says. "They come at dawn."

Jean-Claude, Harlow, and Griim all make for the door, Riven watching them from a standing position behind his desk.

"Wait," I say without turning to face them. "Stop."

"What is it, Everly?" Griim asks.

"Attack me," I say.

"What?" Harlow asks, frowning at me.

"You heard me," I say, brushing my hair back over my shoulder. They forced me into this position and now I'm going to prove a point. Even if it won't do anything to change Riven's mind.

"Everly, this is pointless. We've all already made up our minds on this point," he says as he looks down at me with a scrupulous expression on his face. But I don't care about what he thinks or what he's going to say. My focus is elsewhere.

"Everly," Harlow starts, but Jean-Claude interrupts him.

"We're wasting valuable time," he says.

"It's not a waste," I respond, though I don't argue with him that our time is valuable. It is. And with every passing second, the avenging army from the Academy of Enchantment draws nearer. Our enemies advance, and we stand here squabbling over one little dryad. One little, *powerful* dryad.

"Attack me," I say again. "All three of you. Give me everything you have."

"Everly—" Griim's calm and reasoned voice cuts through the tension, but I don't let him finish.

"The faster you do as I say, the faster we can move on with our plans," I say.

I feel the first man move, sensing his steps with a silent spell of second sight.

Harlow.

The others follow and bear down. I swing around and blast Harlow in the chest with a deflection spell. I shift my weight and elbow Jean-Claude in the jugular. He doesn't have any breath to catch, but he stumbles back in surprise nonetheless. Griim is the only one who remains standing. I summon the energy of nature from the eternal source within me and when Griim approaches me, I smack him down on his ass with a forcefield of kinetic energy.

Then I stand there, facing all of them, hands on my hips and anger in my expression.

Without any warning, Riven comes at me from behind. A blast of powerful magic hits me square in the back and I slam onto the floor. But I'm expecting it so I spin around, on my back, and holding my hands in his direction, I summon *Fortuna*. It's a simple reversal of fortunes spell, but it works like the charm it is.

Riven collapses against the ground as I regain my footing and pull myself up. Stealing myself with a deep breath, I walk over to Riven and, standing in front of him, look down with my hands on my hips.

"Riven, are you okay?" It looks like I hit him with a little too much *Fortuna* and might have knocked him out.

Riven's eyes start to move rapidly back and forth beneath his eyelids. His eyelashes flutter, and when he opens his eyes, he appears dazed, a bit shell-shocked. There's surprise written all over his features. I can't help the pride that wells up within me. I did it—I've proven my point. I defended myself against each one of them.

"Well, he is not dead, thus there is that," Jean-Claude says in a completely bored tone—like this is something that happens every day. While he might not appear especially surprised, the same can't be said for Griim and Harlow.

Harlow paces the room while rubbing his hand up and down the back of his neck like he does when he's upset. And Griim just stands there, facing me with wide eyes. Wide, surprised and impressed eyes.

I told them I was powerful, I think to myself, perhaps with the slightest twinge of smugness. Being a dryad trained in divination, enchantment and necromancy, I'm more multifaceted than most creatures. And I know I can be of use in this battle. I know I can help protect them just as they're so intent to protect me.

"We're in this together," I whisper.

Riven locks eyes with me from the floor. Slowly, he pulls himself up, one hand draped over his knee. He looks at me and breathes out a long sigh.

"Point taken," he says finally.

"So?" I ask, not sure what to make of his words.

He shakes his head. "So, nothing. Yes, you are very strong and capable, Everly, but that still doesn't change the fact that I won't allow you to fight."

"It's for the best," Harlow says as he turns to face me and offers me a smile of consolation that does nothing but further piss me off.

"You need me," I start, anger brewing inside me. "And I want to fight because they're my enemies, too."

"It is decided," Jean-Claude says, his voice clipped. When he looks at me, there's no solace in his expression—there's just truth, hard and cold. "There is no use delaying any further. We must make our preparations, as time is of the utmost essence."

"Very well." Riven dusts himself off. "Gather your brigades, and Everly, do your best to get what you can out of Dorian's book."

I don't say anything because I'm so angry, tears burn my eyes. I understand why they don't want me to fight—that they're just trying to protect me, but I don't accept it. I want to protect them just as much as they want to protect me, and I know I could help the war efforts. I know I could help them if they'd just allow me the chance.

ELEVEN
♀♥♂♂♂♂
Everly

After everyone leaves Riven's office and Pilot escorts us back to Castle Raven Night, Griim walks me through the doors and up to my room. It's his turn to take care of me while the others plan for the coming battle.

And, yes, I'm just as angry as I was earlier.

"It's just not fair," I complain as we take the steps that lead to my bedroom.

Griim breathes in deeply. "I have a feeling I'm going to regret this," he starts.

I look over at him and feel my eyebrows merge in the center of my forehead as I frown. "Regret what?"

He pauses for a few seconds as he studies my face, and I try to figure out what he's going on about. "Regret what?" I repeat.

"Come with me," he answers and extending his hand, I take it before he leads me back down the stairs and into the darkness outside the castle.

"Where are we going?"

"To the armory at Ever Dark."

"The armory?" I repeat, shaking my head. "Why?"

"Because if you're going to fight, you need to wear protection."

###

Ever Dark Academy's armory is astounding, but I'm still overcome with the fact that Griim even brought me here in the first place. He obviously knows he shouldn't be going against Riven's orders and yet, here we are.

'Here' happens to be a circular room of black stone with tunnels leading off in eight different directions from the center. The ceiling is magically fortified glass that changes color, depending on the intent of the person who enters—or, at least, that's what Griim tells me. Now, as we walk inside, it's a soft purple.

"What does it mean that the glass just changed colors from red to purple?" I ask him.

"It means you're pure of heart," Griim answers simply, giving me a smile as he looks down at me. "I'm not surprised. It's the color of your aura."

"My aura?" I ask, fascinated. "I've never seen it before—or any auras, really. I've only read about them in various classes. Are elementals particularly gifted with seeing auras?"

"Not particularly," Griim says on a shrug. "It's more of a familiar trick than anything else. I bet Riddle gets good reads on people, as well. Something about having someone else's soul inside you... it makes you more sensitive to the differences in the fabric that creates each of us."

"That makes sense," I say as I turn to face him. "What color is your aura?"

"Gray."

"Hmm," I laugh. "Do auras always match hair color?"

Griim shakes his head. "No. You and I are special cases."

I glance back up at the ceiling and gesture for Griim to come stand beside me. The ceiling stays perfectly purple, almost a pastel shade in its airy lightness. "I want to thank you for bringing me here," I say to him as I give him a serious expression. "I know you're taking a big risk going against Riven." I pause for a moment or two. "I just... want you to know it means a lot to me."

"You're welcome, Everly," he says on a chuckle.

"Can I ask you something?" I continue.

He nods. "Shoot."

"Why are you risking Riven's anger? Why are you okay with me fighting when everyone else isn't?"

He shrugs, then inhales deeply. "It's not that I'm okay with it."

"Okay…"

"I put myself in your shoes, and I wouldn't have liked it if I felt like everyone was making decisions about me without my input." He smiles down at me. "And I think you made some good points, and you were able to defend yourself against us and… really, we need all the help we can get."

I nod as I look at him. "Well, I appreciate your vote of confidence."

"Just don't die and make me regret it."

I laugh as I nudge him with my elbow. He smiles back and, extending his hand, leads me deeper into the armory.

In the middle of the room, there's a huge sword that appears to be floating. It looks too big for any human to carry, both long and thick, with a strange language carved up the length of the blade. The words glow in an eerie green fluorescence—almost like a light is shining on them, but the glow comes from within the sword. I've never seen anything like it in any books I've read before, nor do I recognize the script from my studies abroad. I look at Griim, curious.

"The Giant's Broadsword," Griim says as he nods to the magnificent piece of weaponry. It has a ruby handle with a single large emerald at its base. I want to reach out and grab it, but restrain myself. I'm here for armor. Not a giant sword.

"Where did it come from?" I ask, still intrigued with the thing.

"It was a peace offering from Brutus the Mighty after the Great War of the Academies," he says.

The Great War of the Academies was so long ago, it's almost like a legend now—one of those things that was rumored to have happened, but you're never sure if it really did. But maybe this is proof? All I know about it is that after that war, the giants retired to the mountains outside of Blue Water and kept to themselves.

"You mean..." I look from Griim to the sword. "The sword is *hundreds* of years old?"

"It was given to Riven from the King of Giants himself," says Griim with a nod. "Offerings of peace don't come often or easily from their kind. Giants are notoriously difficult."

"I can imagine," I say, and imagine is all I can do. I've never met a giant before. I don't even know much about them, really. They tend to keep to their own unless pushed. Since the war, they've kept to their mountains almost entirely. To see one is like catching sight of a shooting star. A shooting star that probably wants to kill you. There are legends of giants eating our kind, but who knows how true those legends are,

"So," I say with a shrug. "Where do we start? Where's the armor?" I look around myself, but don't notice anything that could pass for armor. The room is pretty bare. "It's not much of an armory without any armor."

"True enough," Griim says as he then points through one of the tunnels. "Just through there."

He leads the way down the corridor. At the end, there's another expansive room. True to Griim's promise, this room is full of armor—metal and leather accoutrements appear all over the walls, some in glass cases and others just hanging by pegs, but that's not all. In the far corner of the square room sits an old woman, rocking back and forth as she reclines back into her chair and appears, for all intents and purposes, completely out of place.

"Oh, hullo!" she says. Her voice is old and scratchy.

She stands up, a mess of red and green raggedy clothes. Her head is a mop of silver curls; her face all wrinkles. There's an unquestionable air of frenetic energy about her—like she's made of static. But there's a bright smile on her cherubic face and she seems pleased to see us. I have to wonder how often she gets visitors down here. Probably more so since all of this happened between the Academy of Enchantment and Ever Dark. That makes me wonder why the room isn't busy with students at the moment. As far as I can tell, all those enrolled in Ever Dark are also now part of the war efforts. Therefore, I'd think this place would be in high demand.

"Um…" I say. "Hello. I'm Everly." I extend a hand.

She hobbles up to me and takes my hand, pumping it excitedly. She only comes up to my shoulders, but her arms are surprisingly strong, spindly little things that they are. She must be some sort of hobgoblin, maybe? Or a sprite? There aren't a whole lot of creatures who are smaller than I am.

I glance back at Griim and find him wearing a wide smile as he runs his hands through his shaggy hair and crosses his arms over his chest.

With a nod at the tiny old beetle of a woman in front of me, he says, "Everly, I now have the unparalleled honor of introducing you to Ever Dark Academy's resident seamstress, Dolores."

"That's me!" Dolores calls out and then beams at both of us as though she's some sort of celebrity and we should be honored just to be in her company. And for all I know, maybe she is.

"Seamstress?" I repeat, frowning. I'm just not really sure what she's doing in an armory that seems like it gets next to no business. "Where is everyone?" I ask, as I look around.

"Ye just missed the rush," she answers and gives me another gap-tooth smile. "Aye, but they'll be back, they will. When war is on the horizon, ye need all the protection ye can get, nae?"

I look at the little creature up and down again, this time with greater focus. I'm not sure what sort of creature she is, yet, I'm hesitant to ask. Usually, it's rude to ask someone's magical identity. I figure I could use *Identify*, but the subject doesn't really matter enough to me. Besides, I'm here to get some armor, not make new friends.

"Dolores has been at the school for as long as I can remember," Griim says, as if reading my mind. "And she's really a blessing because she can assure your armor is the right one for you."

Dolores barrels over to Griim and wraps him in a hug and I can't help but smile. He gives her three soft pats on the head, and she releases him. Griim shakes his head and smiles at me, evidently seeing my confusion written plainly on my face.

He sidles over to me as Dolores makes her way slowly back to the rocking chair. There's a strange-looking spinning wheel beside her—something I didn't notice before, probably because my attention was wrapped up on Dolores. Now, as I study the wheel, it reminds me of something from Rumpelstiltskin. She leans it forward and rests the needle point on her knee. I turn to Griim.

"What is she?" I ask as quietly as humanly possible.

"Dolores is a genuine human," Griim says. A human? But that's... that's impossible! Humans have been extinct since long before I was born.

"A human?!"

When I raise my eyebrows in disbelief, Griim adds a quick, "It's true."

"No way," I say. "What's a human doing in Dread?"

"What's a dryad doing in Dread?" he asks, quirking an eyebrow.

"Touché," I respond as my eyes seek out the strange spinning wheel and its stranger operator. A human. I've only heard about them in textbooks and from stories passed down over the centuries. "I'd be fascinated to know how she found herself here at Ever Dark Academy." I swallow hard. "And, furthermore, how is she even still alive?" As far as I know, humans live to be about eighty or ninety, if they're lucky but the last human (as far as I knew) died out over two hundred years ago. How this one is still alive... it must be magic.

"Ah, that would be magic that's been keeping her alive all this time," Griim answers. Then he looks at Dolores with a fond smile. "We have come for armor, Dolores," he says.

"You know the rules, young Griim," Dolores says. "You must solve my riddles three, or leaving empty-handed you will be."

"Do we have time for riddles?" I whisper to him, thinking the answer is a resounding 'no'.

"Dolores is the keeper of the armor, thus we have to play by her rules," he answers as I nod and face her again. I don't know if I'm any good at riddles because I've never been asked one before. Guess we are soon to find out.

"Give us the first riddle, please," Griim says.

Dolores sits up straight in her chair. Then she slowly rises and hovers a few inches above the seat of the chair in a feat of very unhumanlike ability. Or, at least, that's what I've been told of humans—that they possess no magic. So how…

It's almost like she's possessed because there's a sudden expression on her face that wasn't there before—almost like there's a face within her face. And I could swear her eyes went from brown to bright green.

I turn to Griim. The look on his face tells me my suspicions are correct. The human Dolores isn't the only one occupying that little body. Dolores is infected with a ghost, I'm pretty sure anyway.

"How long has she been possessed?" I ask Griim quietly.

"As long as I've known her," he answers on a shrug. "But the spirit isn't malevolent. It simply comes and goes. It's responsible for the riddles."

"The ghost speaks the riddles?" I ask, surprised.

He nods. "It's a strange spirit."

"How did it possess her?" I ask. "Nonhuman spirits usually need to be summoned by someone, a Druid or a warlock or—"

"Very true," Griim says. "And it was a Druid."

Dolores' eyes go glassy and her face turns sallow. She suddenly looks so much older, borderline dead actually. Her jaw slowly unhinges and she lets her mouth fall open too wide.

"I speak without a mouth and hear without ears," Dolores says, but her voice is that of a gruff old man rather than herself. I look at Griim, worried, but he gives me a reassuring nod as if he's experienced this exact situation numerous times. And, for all I know, maybe he has.

"I have no body, but I come alive with wind," Dolores goes on. "What am I?"

Griim gives me a look that says he's expecting me to come up with the answer. "Let's see," I say as I face him. "What speaks without a mouth and hears without ears? What has no body but comes alive with wind?" I repeat, mainly for myself.

"That's a tricky one," he says, shaking his head and breathing in deeply. He seems concerned.

"How many guesses do we get?" I ask.

"One," Dolores's man voice crones. "One for each of you."

"Is it always like this when students come to get armor?" I ask Griim.

"Only if you're new," he answers. "Once you go through this initiation ritual, you'll never have to answer another of Dolores' riddles."

"But in the wake of a coming war, do we really have time for this?"

He nods. "Time is standing still, Everly, and has been since we entered the armory. It's how Dolores is still here and why she can never leave this cave. Time doesn't exist here."

I run the words through my mind in complete shock and then remind myself I have a riddle I still need to solve. Griim mutters part of the riddle over again, under his breath, fixating on the portion about the wind.

"I'm blanking," he admits with a shrug.

I squint at Dolores, thinking hard. Her silver hair floats up around her and frizzes in all directions. Her hanging jaw swings a bit back and forth, but the rest of her is completely frozen.

I suddenly hear the sound of water dripping— the sound reverberates through the tunnel from the central sword display and the answer to her riddle is suddenly obvious.

"An echo," I say. "It's an echo."

Dolores's head turns toward the ceiling slowly. Her bones make an agonizing creaking sound as she moves her head. It looks like she's trying to nod.

"You got it," Griim says. He looks at me, golden eyes alight with wonder and amusement.

"Brilliant. You're a lot more than just a pretty face, you know that?"

"I'm also an expert riddle-solver, apparently."

We chuckle, and Dolores' jaw starts another slow trek upwards. It moves like it's made of water that flows in slow motion.

"What word in the English language does the following?" Dolores' man voice asks. "The first two letters signify a male, the first three letters signify a female, the first four letters together mean 'a great man', while the entire word means 'a great woman'. What is the word?"

Griim sets his jaw and stares at Dolores with intensity. He plants his hands on his hips and bites his lower lip.

"First two letters signify a male," I say. And then something occurs to me. "Wait, do I have to answer all these questions on my own? Since this is my first time in the armory?" I turn to face Dolores as I wait for an answer.

She shakes her head. "Griim may assist you."

I nod as I return my attention to Griim. "Thank the goddess for that."

"He," Griim says. "The first two letters that signify a man are 'he'." I nod. "And the first three letters signify a female," I continue.

"Her," Griim says.

"The first for letters mean a great man," I continue.

"A hero," Griim says as a huge smile overcomes his features and we both turn to face Dolores, who simply nods.

"I got it!" Griim says. "Heroine! The English word is Heroine!"

Dolores does her creepy ceiling nod again and Griim looks at me, a proud glint in his golden eye. We both turn to look at Dolores then, the final riddle on the tip of her dry, cracked lips.

"A girl has as many brothers as sisters, but each brother has only half as many brothers as sisters. How many brothers and sisters are there in the family?"

I close my eyes as I consider the last of the riddles. I can see the words turning into images in my head—images of brothers and sisters. As I run the words through my mind, I open my eyes and immediately announce: "Four sisters and three brothers."

"Damn!" Griim looks visibly impressed. "That was fast! I didn't know you were such a mathematician."

"What can I say?" I shrug with a laugh. "I'm full of surprises."

With that, Dolores drops from the air. She hits the chair and slumps into it, her hair falling in her face. It's like all the lifeforce has been sucked from her body by an invisible blackhole. I take a step toward her to make sure she's all right, but Griim stops me with a hand on my shoulder.

"Don't worry," he says. "She'll be right in a minute."

"But it looks like she's dead, Griim." I argue, gesturing at her slumped body. As far as I can tell, she isn't breathing.

"Just give her a second," he says in a calming voice. "She'll be all right. Dolores has been around a long time."

Sure enough, Dolores's tiny body slowly but surely starts to lift itself into a sitting position. Her eyes are back to their original color, and a blush has returned to her face. When she looks up, she gives us both a shy smile.

With that, she gathers a bundle of what appears to be finely woven gold thread sitting on the floor at her side. There's a whole basket full of it. Then she feeds the golden thread into the spinning wheel and as the wheel starts spinning, she feeds it more and more of the gold thread. As I watch, the thread turns under and over on itself, spinning this way and that until it plops out a piece of coarsely braided chainmail. The armor is heavy and falls off the wheel with a loud clunk as it lands on the ground.

"How is that… possible?" I ask.

"It's an enchanted spinning wheel," Griim explains. "It's been at Ever Dark Academy forever."

"Just like Dolores?"

"Just like Dolores," he confirms.

She continues to work for a short time longer, maybe close to ten minutes. We, meanwhile, walk over to stand directly in front of the spinning wheel to watch her work. Her fingers are quick and nimble as they help to spin the machine and as she spins, she hums a tune I don't recognize. She doesn't say anything more but her humming is somehow soothing. After another ten minutes or so, another piece of clothing turns out from the wheel and plops on the floor. This one appears to be a tunic of dark brown linen. She continues to spin and then lifts the final piece of clothing for me to expect.

This looks like long-sleeved shoulder pads made of black leather that cover the chest and back areas. Each one with studded with metal fasteners. I'm surprised to find it looks exactly my size.

"Wow," I say. "She really is an artist."

"Try it on," Griim says.

I slip the tunic over my clothes. It hugs my body like a glove. Movement is as easy as if I were wearing nothing at all. Then I follow it with the chainmail and then the leather shoulder pad things.

It's heavy but not unbearable and I definitely feel more protected than I did when we first walked in. The two of us walk toward the tunnel that leads back to the center of the armory.

TWELVE
♀♥♂♂♂♂
Everly
Two Days Later

Our army gathers at the front wall of the school.

The dark, volcanic and mountainous terrain will be helpful during battle. Our warriors are adorned in their armor and everyone is prepared, but on edge, as is to be expected. Everyone is decked out in the armory's finest. The elementals carry their elements with them for battle fodder. The vampires hold shields and bare their fangs, readying themselves to deflect wooden stakes from the Academy of Enchantment's army. The incubi look the most frightening in their natural form—all of them with red and shining skin, wings, horns and tails. They brandish broadswords and flails, experts at violence.

"Arcadia's army is coming," Riven says, holding a finger to his throat to magnify his voice with a spell. "Ready yourselves."

"Everly," Griim says. He pushes through a crowd of elementals and makes his way over to me. We were separated for a time after our trip to the armory because he needed to prepare his brigade. But now, he's here, dressed in his armor.

And I'm here too, standing in front of Riven, but he doesn't recognize me owing to my *Camouflage* spell which changes my outward appearance.

"Stay close to me, okay?" Griim asks. There's anxiety in his voice and intensity on his face. "You remember all your spells, right?" he asks nervously. "*Deflect, Defend*—"

"*Double Back* if they gang up on me," I finish for him, giving him a smile even though I'm so nervous, my voice shakes. "I remember."

"Good," he says, then repeats himself. "Good." He gets a strange look in his eyes, like he's distracted and troubled. Not that I can blame him. We're soon to be up against Arcadia's best—a legion of Centaur soldiers as well as whatever enchanted beings the school was able to provide. This will be a fight to remember, I'm certain of that.

Griim pulls away and grabs me by the chin. "You be careful out there," he says. There's worry in his eyes and I'm sure it reflects the worry in my own.

"I will be," I say with a clipped nod. "You too."

The two of us part ways then, though remaining in each other's eyeline. Griim stands at the front of the elemental brigade, arranged in a triangular formation with the other factions of the army. Jean-Claude and Harlow stand on either side of him, a great distance away, separated by soldiers. And I hover behind them, immersed in the mass of bodies that loom before the castle.

"Stand at attention!" Riven calls, and the warriors all straighten their spines and prepare to charge the craggy open field of rock that stretches out in front of us.

Over the horizon, I see what looks like a line of black static moving towards us in front of the rising sun.

"They're here," I say to myself and my heartbeat picks up, now beating even faster than it was before. I suddenly wish I had Riddle here to comfort me, but Griim and I decided it wouldn't be a good place for the little guy—he'd be too easy a target. So he's back inside my bedroom at Castle Raven Night and I can only hope I'll be lucky enough to see him again.

You will survive this, I tell myself resolutely and then I think of all my friends and the worry returns doubly. *All of them will.*

I steel my resolve and lift my hands in front of me, ready to start casting. The little black line becomes a series of larger moving shapes, and the advancing army takes form. There are legions of centaurs, the fae, and light sorcerers and all of them are coming right at us.

Riven lifts his finger to his throat. He commands the army forward.

We charge.

They start pouring forth, students upon students with no training under their belts, save what they learned in classes. They brandish all sorts of weapons, screaming at the top of their lungs, and sprinting straight into the line of fire.

I come to blows with an orange-skinned coral sprite. She swings a pickaxe at my neck, but I dodge by an inch and a half. I blast her with a defensive spell, and she goes careening into the midsection of a thinly set centaur who tumbles to the ground with her, hoofs flailing in the air.

I catch sight of Harlow out of the corner of my eye. He's locked in a heated battle with a light sorcerer. His army moves in violent throngs, crashing forward like waves against the morning shore. Jean-Claude is no worse off. He's grappling with a member of the fae whose race I can't get a clear read on. Her ears are pointy like a faerie, but she's got the sparkling skin of a nymph. In my peripherals, I see Jean-Claude sink his pointed fangs into the soft skin of the creature's neck. She screams, the sound piercing through the air amid the clash of weapons, sound of shouting, and the overall cacophony that surrounds us all.

Someone unseen lands a blow to my side. There's a sudden sharp sting in the right side of my abdomen and it winds me momentarily. Clutching my side, I spin around, an offensive spell locked and loaded.

"*Defend*," I start, but when I turn to see who's hit me, I only see a stout man's dead body, covered in his own blood, clutching a broadsword in his meaty fist.

I look up and see Harlow. He's standing over the man, chest heaving. He leans down, plucks the sword from the dead man, and hands it to me. From the expression in his eyes, he doesn't recognize me.

The *Camouflage* spell is still working. I nod to him in thanks and take the sword with both hands. It's heavier than it looks, but I manage to keep it upright. We lock eyes in the middle of the chaos and he studies me with a strange expression on his face, as if he isn't sure who it is that stands before me.

"I don't know how the hell you managed this," he growls as his eyes narrow and he grabs me by the arm. He pulls me into him so I can hear him shout in my ear. "But it's too late for arguments now." He pauses. "Don't be afraid to spill blood," he continues. "Violence can be a great accompaniment to magic."

I nod and lift the sword. He gives my split side a worried once over, placing his hand gingerly over the seeping wound. I wince and watch when he pulls his hands away, it's soaked in my blood.

"I'm okay," I tell him. "The wound isn't deep."

The wound is deep, but I'm fairly sure it doesn't reach the bone and doesn't seem to have hit any vital organs. That means, I can keep fighting. Before Harlow can argue, a team of centaurs in a diamond formation charge us from the far side of the rocky field.

"Get behind me!" Harlow says, but I step out in front of him and, dropping down to my haunches, I reach out, placing my hands on the earth. Then I inhale deeply, sucking in all the natural essence of the environment that I can manage. The more power I have to start with, the more I can safely expend. Of course, I'm not too worried about what's safe and what isn't. In the middle of this battle, in the middle of screaming and dying warriors who are all too young to sacrifice something as precious as their own lives, I'm only worried about keeping our soldiers alive.

"Everly!" Harlow tries to pull me up. "What are you doing? We've got to move!"

A soft purple light emanates from my hands, almost as if the energy I absorbed is leaking out of me because it simply has nowhere else to go. I stand back up to full height and look the leading centaur dead in the face. He seems familiar, and I wonder if he was one of the men who attacked me when I was at the Academy of Enchantment. In any case, he's coming for me now, and that leaves me with only one option.

I join my wrists in front of me and tighten my jaw. With all the strength in my body, I thrust my arms forward. The blast of pure purple light that shoots from my hands surprises me because it's stronger, more powerful, than I'd anticipated.

The lead centaur's eyes widen. He starts to rear back, to lead his soldiers away, but it's too late. The light latches around his neck and rapidly crushes the air out of his half-horse body. Shards of light break off from the main beam like pieces of exploding glass. They shoot off, acting as projectiles into the hearts, necks, cheeks, arms, legs, and—in one gnarly case—eyes of the others just beside and behind him.

I cringe at the sight and sprint in the other direction, Harlow's leather-clad ass still on my heels. I can't believe he's wearing that stupid jacket over his kevlar. It seems like it would impede his movements, but Harlow, it seems, doesn't go anywhere without his leather jacket. War is apparently no exception.

In the distance, past Harlow's spread-out terrain of incubus territory where his students violently destroy the incoming enemy, I see a single figure atop the horizon line.

"Who is that?" I yell to Harlow, blocking a blow from a flail with my sword. I just saved my lower left thigh from a brutal beating.

Harlow's gaze follows my finger to where I point. He squints, but there's no trace of recognition or understanding in his eyes. He doubles back to slice a nymph across the shoulder with his blade, then spins back to my side in a fluid move. I didn't expect Harlow to be such a graceful warrior, but the elegant lines of his finely made body move as if he was created for battle.

Harlow and I are quickly separated. I'm jostled away in a gaggle of other fighters from Ever Dark Academy. He charges into a cluster of light workers whose spells are no match for the frenzy of violence that Harlow comes to deliver. He cuts them all down like weeds in a briar patch. It's an awful sight, but I can't look away. Unfortunately, I need to.

Just in time to get clubbed in the forehead by the hilt of an oncoming sword, I spin around and hit the ground. There's a fresh pulsing pain blossoming in the muscles that broke my fall. I raise my head and stare through my hair at the horizon line once more. Whoever hit me is gone, and the skyline before me is completely clear. For some reason, that knowledge cuts through my adrenaline and sends a chill up my spine.

Jean-Claude pulls me up off the ground with one hand on my wrist. I barely recognize him, he's so covered in blood. But he recognizes me. I figure, in the conjuring of that light blast, I must have disrupted the *Camouflage* spell, so now I look like myself again. Oh, well. It's not as though they can send me back to the castle now.

Jean-Claude's eyes are frenzied. And that is truly a sight to behold because it goes against everything I've ever known about him. He's usually so calm and collected. Now, he's every bit the feral monster people fear vampires to be, and yet, I'm not afraid of him because I know his feelings for me and I know I can always rely on him to keep me safe.

Another brigade of centaurs emerges from the end of the field. I hear a blood-curdling roar from behind me and spin around. And what I see shocks me to the core.

A dragon.

"What… what is that?" I say, in awe as I watch the creature breathe a line of fire all the way around him, destroying everything in his proximity.

"That is Cackus," Jean-Claude answers, pride in his tone.

Cackus, the dragon, swats away a series of light workers and woodland sprites who descend on him with a flick of his enormous and scaled tail. They scatter like crumbs dusted off the top of a table. I just continue to stand there, amazed by the sight before me. Cackus is just so incredibly fierce and much larger than I would've guessed.

He towers nearly to the top of the tallest spire in the mountainous castle. The top of his head is adorned with three rows of increasingly massive horns. His scaly red skin almost glows in the light of the moon. He's absolutely breathtaking, and as the rest of the enemy legion takes notice of him, for the first few moments, they're too stunned to carry on with the carnage. It's as though the battle is suddenly set on pause and everyone's attention is riveted by the dragon.

Suddenly, I see a man emerge from the horizon line.

At first, I don't recognize him.

But at second glance, I see the man for what he is. A light Druid.

The rarest of all sorcerers.

There's only one light Druid in every thousand Druids, who are a rare race all on their own. I've never seen one in real life, but I've read about them and seen pictures. I know the crystal blue robe of ceremonial purity, the white, glassy eyes, the features that seem to hint at the man being both immortal and on the very precipice of death. A paradox unto himself, something unintended by the natural world, but powerful as all hell, nonetheless.

So just as we have our own hidden surprise in Cackus, they have the same in the light Druid. Our secret weapons are about to get pitted against each other.

To my abject horror, the light Druid lifts his hands and the gray clouds in the sky open up, as though torn clean down the middle like a sheet of paper. Viscous shades of blue, green and purple pulse above the open tear. As I watch, stardust swirls in their depths, and for a second, I'm too enchanted by the sight to even be frightened.

"Everly!" Griim appears at my side and, reaching out, grabs my hand. "We've gotta go!" he yells.

I take his hand, and we run. Only for a second. The last second.

At the sound of a whistling through the air, I turn my head in time to see a centaur as he lets loose an arrow. It almost feels like slow motion as I watch the arrow travel straight past me as it impales Griim's chest.

"No!" I scream.

And then I'm suddenly falling down to my knees at the same time Griim does. I catch him against me and a second later, he simply crumbles to dust in my arms as if he never was a person at all.

"No..." I repeat, my voice much softer this time.

He can't die, I remind myself. *He's a familiar.*

I look to Cackus for assurance that Griim's going to be all right. If Cackus is still alive, Griim can be brought back.

Just then, I see Jean-Claude headed straight for the light sorcerer. The Druid flings a beam of pure white magic at him, and Jean-Claude simply lifts his enchanted shield to deflect it. But the Druid's power is too much and travels through the shield, entering Jean-Claude, who suddenly begins to glow. He drops the shield and clutches his heart as he falls to the ground and I hear myself screaming his name.

Cackus then turns his attention to the Druid and, heaving a mighty breath, blows an impressive mouthful of bellowing flame at the sorcerer. The Druid responds by covering himself with a shield of blue light, beating the flames back.

As soon as Cackus breathes in again, no doubt to furnish another onslaught of flames, the Druid throws his hands forward and millions of ice blades come flying from his palms. They surround Cackus, but rather than piercing his scales, they simply begin to join one another, looking like a glowing, supernatural net that surrounds him. As I watch, the net encloses him fully and then begins pulling him upwards.

The dragon is yanked straight up into the sky, directly above the light Druid. Cackus appears to notice him and swats down a massive claw which pierces the Druid through his midsection. At that exact moment, the Druid releases an incredibly bright light that pierces Cackus in turn, and flows right through him. The dragon rears back in obvious agony as the loudest of all bellows echoes from him. A second or so later, his eyes go dim and his neck droops. A few seconds more and he starts falling from the sky and directly into a circular portal that appears directly below him. Inside, the portal appears to be spinning stars of all different colors.

Everyone on the battlefield watches in stunned silence as both our most powerful players disappear into the Druid's open portal. As soon as the portal absorbs them both, it closes and disappears entirely.

I turn around to take in all the shocked expressions around me. But my attention doesn't remain on the soldiers for long. Instead, it falls to the clay mound at my feet that used to be Griim.

But Griim is gone.

And Cackus isn't here to bring him back.

I fall to my knees, cutting them both on the hard stone surface, and sob into the black rocks below me.

THIRTEEN
♀♥♂♂♂♂
Jean-Claude

I carry Everly through the bodies strewn about the field as I force myself forward, towards Castle Raven Night.

Her head lolls to the side with exhaustion. Her face is swollen with tears, her eyes shut tight. Tears trickle through her tightly clenched eyelids, no matter how hard she fights them. And I cannot fault her for them.

Who could have guessed the Druid would open a portal to another realm and that he would take Cackus with him? Of course, I know not where Cackus ended up—perhaps in some liminal space between our world and the next. There is no telling, for certain. But what is of great concern was the appearance of the Druid at all—he was an unknown to us—a sign that the Academy of Enchantment was awaiting this opportunity. They were grooming him for this exact reason.

As to Griim, with no one here to reanimate him, namely Cackus, he is as good as gone forever. Or until Cackus is returned to us, if indeed the old dragon is still alive. And that is anyone's guess.

As if hearing the thought in my mind, Everly releases a bone-chilling sob. She clutches at the fabric of my cloak. Her fingers are white with the effort of holding on, almost as though she worries she will slip away into nothingness if she releases me. For a moment, I am stupid enough to hope she never does let go. At least for now, in this exact moment, she is close to me, which means I know she is safe.

I am still in disbelief that she even fought in the battle at all, though even as the thought crosses my mind, I realize I have misjudged her. She is stubborn, and she is determined, and I should have known she would thwart Riven's orders. I cannot fault her for it, and I am not angry.

I am just relieved to have her here, in my arms, and to know she is alive.

"Everything will be alright, Everly," I tell her, even as I doubt my own words. We might have won this battle, but that means nothing because it will now simply be a matter of time before Granger rebuilds his defenses and attacks us again.

And I hesitate whether to even call this battle a victory—as soon as the Druid and Cackus disappeared, the centaurs called off their attack. They simply retreated, but I do not feel as if the victory was awarded to us. I wonder if this was their intention all along—surprise us with an attack, just so they could get to Cackus? I was not certain whether Granger knew of Cackus, but now I must believe he did.

Regardless, we have lost one of our best. Thus, we are weak, and Granger will use that weakness to his advantage.

Preternaturally slowly, Everly lifts her head from my chest and looks me dead in the face. There is venom in her eyes and her expression is one I have never seen her wear before. She appears to be furious with me, and I am quite stunned.

"Don't you dare say it's alright," she says, shaking her head as the tears continue to bleed from her lovely eyes. "Griim is *gone*." She chokes on the last word as if there is a frog caught in her throat. The sound pulls at my undead heartstrings.

"I am sorry, Everly," I say.

###
Harlow

I knock three times on Everly's door.

The sound of racking sobs stops, but I can hear Everly as she sniffles loudly. Then she climbs off the bed with a soft creak, her footsteps making it clear she's on her way slowly to the door. She hesitates there. I hear her ragged breathing as she inhales deeply and unlatches the lock.

The door swings inward.

Her eyes are puffy and red. She looks drained of all vitality, her life force stripped away. Her lovely lavender hair is frizzy and matted. She's been crying into her pillow for a while. I can see the moist indentation in the thing from the corner of my eye.

"What are you doing here?" she croaks.

I lift the bottle of whiskey I swiped from Riven's office.

"Peace offering," I say with a wry smile.

She sighs, rolls her eyes, and walks back toward the bed. "Not interested," she mumbles over her shoulder. "Nothing, alcohol included, is going to take this pain away." She breathes in deeply, then looks over at me. "Can you shut the door on your way out?"

She flops back on the bed.

I enter the room and close the door by kicking it with one foot. She doesn't look up when I make my way over to her side of the bed. "I'm not leaving, Everly," I say. "You need company right now."

She looks at me and even though she doesn't say anything, her eyes are haunted. She doesn't want me here but, like I said, I'm not going to leave. She needs someone—she needs *me*.

"I wanted to first apologize," I start.

"What for?"

"Because I'm disappointed in myself for how I acted when we first got you back from the Academy of Enchantment."

She looks at me and her lips are tight, her eyes narrowed. "Don't ever mention those words to me again." She breathes in deeply. "Just call it 'the academy'." She shakes her head. "Enchantment," she says and then laughs without humor.

I nod as if to tell her I understand her feelings—the hatred and anger that's currently plaguing her. "Anyway, I was eager for you to get your memories back, and I didn't have a thought for how losing them would affect you." I breathe in deeply. "I know I put a lot of pressure and stress on you and it wasn't fair. I'm sorry for that."

"It doesn't matter, Harlow," she says. "None of it matters anymore," she continues, shaking her head. "It's over now. Griim is dead. None of it matters."

"You're wrong," I tell her as gently as I can. "There are still things that matter. You're safe and your life matters…"

"Does my life matter more than Griim's did?" she asks, bitterness tinging her voice. "Does my life matter more than any of the people who lost their lives in that battle today? Is my life worth all the pain this stupid war caused? Is it worth the heartache?"

I reach for her hand but stop myself. She flinches away.

"Yes," I say simply. "Yes, Everly, your life is worth every drop of blood spilled and every life lost, Griim's included. Your life is worth all of it and I know the others would agree, especially Griim."

She scoffs and sits right up to look me in the eye, and even though she wants to fight the truth in my words, I can see that she can't. She knows the truth in them just as much as I do.

She looks at me thoughtfully then, more tears brimming her eyes. Then she sniffles and wipes her nose on the back of her arm. She shifts her body slightly to face me more directly. "Have you ever lost someone you loved?"

It isn't a question I was expecting, but I answer it, nonetheless. "Yes."

"Who was it?"

"I lost my best friend when I was seventeen."

"You did?" She looks concerned. Dryads are so caring and compassionate by nature. Even after everything she's experienced—all the loss she's currently facing, I can see the compassion and concern she has for me in her eyes.

I simply nod.

"What happened to…"

"Her," I finish for her. "Her name was Chrysanthemum. She was an incubus, like me."

"What happened to her?" she repeats.

I'm not sure where to start and it's a subject I haven't thought about or talked about in the longest time. No one has cared enough to listen, and despite the years that have passed since Chrissy died, some days the pain still feels too raw to openly discuss—on the days I let the memories revisit me, anyway. Usually, I don't. Usually, I keep them locked away. Apparently, today isn't one of those days.

"She fell in love with a fae woman," I say on a shrug. "And they had a love affair for the history books." I recall Chrissy's face, her hardy disposition. "Chrissy was utterly unique." I give Everly a long glance. "Like someone else I know."

Everly looks down, an unwilling blush stealing up to her cheeks.

"She was strong, a fierce warrior," I tell her, remembering my friend fondly with only a slight twinge of grief.

"Tell me more about her."

I nod. "Chrissy hated it when people called her by her full name—which was why she went by 'Chrissy'. She hated pretty much everything, actually. She was always annoyed but funny as all hell. The only person she'd let call her Chrysthanthemum was Elena. Elena was her exception to everything."

"She sounds like an interesting woman," Everly says kindly. "I'm sorry you lost her."

"My grief was nothing compared to what Elena went through," I say with a shake of my head. I remember watching sobs wracking Elena's body for hours on end, days, then weeks into months and even years. Eventually, I had to walk away or I'd get taken in by all the grief—I never would have been able to heal. Even now, I wonder if I am truly healed or if I just shoved the memories away where I wouldn't have to face them. Maybe I never truly processed Chrissy's death.

"What was Elena like?"

"She was pretty exceptional, I have to admit," I say. "Elena was gorgeous, the kind of gorgeous you read about in mythic novels and shit." I take a breath and let it out again—I don't like living in the world of memories because most of mine aren't good ones. "She was gentle and kind and soft like a dove but so fragile."

"Fragile?" Everly asks.

"When Chrissy died, Elena went off the deep end," I say honestly. "Watching her fall apart was almost as hard as losing Chris."

"How did you lose Chrissy?" she asks, tenderness in her gaze. I want to drown in it, take her hand and feel everything she has to offer. But I refrain.

"She killed herself."

Everly is silent.

I am too.

"I'm so sorry," she says. "Did she ever say why?"

"She left a note," I answer on a nod. "Her reasons didn't have anything to do with me or Elena. She wanted that made clear. It was some irreconcilable family drama. Her birth parents were real pieces of work, and... well, the truth was that Chrissy was always a bit off."

"Off how?"

"Just... off in her own world, you know?" I ask, shaking my head. "Chrissy had a mind of her own and it was filled with turmoil. She was born a troubled succubus and then made more troubled by the world around her."

"That's terrible," Everly says. She hugs her arms tightly around herself. "It must've been so devastating to lose her."

"It was." I swallow firmly and look her full in the face. "But I got through it," I tell her with a nod and an understanding smile. "And you will too—with all of this—you'll get through it eventually, Everly. You're stronger than you think."

"I don't feel like I am."

"I know you are." I roll the whiskey bottle between my hands thoughtfully.

"The pain is just so heavy, Harlow," she says as she shakes her head. "It's like I don't know what to do with it—how to handle the fact that *he's* gone."

"You deal with it day by day and each day it gets a little easier," I answer.

"I hope... I hope you're right." She swallows and then makes tepid eye contact with me. "Thanks for staying and for... helping me through this."

I hold up the whiskey bottle. "You shouldn't thank me yet. Not until you partake in some gut rot—that will probably help you way more than I can."

She laughs, and then just looks at me for a moment, shaking her head. "Are you just trying to get in my pants?"

It's a fair question, given what I am, but the answer isn't quite so simple.

"Everly, if you asked me never to touch you again, I would never lay another finger on you. It's enough just to be in your presence." She frowns up at me, but I shake my head. "Really—I'm being honest. You mean that much to me."

"I never know what to say when you say things like that," she admits.

"Then don't say anything," I tell her on a shrug. "I know you're hurting right now, and I'm only here to help."

I hold up the bottle of whiskey again. "I know your sorrows can swim, but it's fun to try drowning them, anyway."

She gives me an almost imperceptible nod.

I uncork the whiskey bottle and because I don't see any cups in the vicinity, I hand her the whole bottle.

FOURTEEN
♀♥♂♂♂♂
Everly

"Goddess, I miss Griim, Harlow," I say.

"I know you do."

But I don't think he understands the extent of the pain plowing through me. Yes, he's lost someone close to him, but that was a long time ago. And, as far as I know, Harlow doesn't have any close friends at Ever Dark. He has his brother, of course, but I'm not so sure how close they are— I've never met his brother, anyway.

"It feels like someone's pulled my heart out of my chest and shoved it back down my throat," I explain.

"At least it wasn't up your ass," Harlow says jokingly.

I don't laugh. I just can't bring myself to feel anything close to joy when my heart is so hollow, so full of pain.

I sort of can't believe that my comfort in my time of grief is Harlow, of all people. "Comfort" might not be the right word, though. I'm not exactly comforted by him, just more distracted, distracted from the big ugly pulsing ball of hatred and rage that's sunk into the pit of my gut.

"I want them to pay for this," I say, my teeth clenching as my hands ball into fists.

"Who? Arcadia?"

"All of them—Arcadia, Granger, the Academy of Enchantment," I answer. "I want them to pay."

"Revenge won't bring him back, Everly."

"Don't you think I know that?" I demand as I look at him and frown.

Hot tears bubble up over my lashline.

I can't fight them back. I don't have the strength or even the desire to maintain my composure. My body is wracked with sobs. I hold myself tightly, clutching at my own arms. I shake hard.

"You're even beautiful when you cry, you know that?" Harlow asks, voice husky. He lies back against the pillows at the head of the bed and stretches his arm out, gesturing for me to come lie beside him. I'm too weak and depressed to argue, so I lean down against him.

His leather jacket slides against the soft material of the pillows. I nestle into his muscular arms and rest my head on his shoulder and my hand on his stomach. While it feels good to be close to him, it doesn't do anything for the pain inside me.

"I can take your pain away, you know…" he says to break the silence.

His eyes are hooded and smoky. I feel his breath on my skin like the stifling humidity of a hot day. Despite myself, his powers of seduction take over my physiology. I lean into him slightly. My cheeks flush. My warm, wet tears trickle down to my chin.

"Please, Everly," Harlow asks, sounding like a starving man begging for bread. "I can't stand to see you like this. Please, let me take the pain away…"

He puts a large, warm hand on my knee, and I don't stop him.

"Your skin is soft," he whispers as he brings his nose to my neck and inhales deeply.

A single tear falls from my eye and courses down my cheek.

Harlow stops his ministrations and goes still as a statue. "Do you want me to take the pain, Everly?"

I'm torn by the question.

Do I want him to take the pain away? Of course, I do. I'd give anything to make this relentless emptiness go away. But, then again,

Griim is gone forever and now all I have left of him are the memories and the memories are the pain. The pain is all I have left of him. And if Harlow took that pain away, would I forget him altogether? Would it be like the purging the Academy of Enchantment did to me to eradicate Dread from my mind? I don't know.

The truth is, I don't really care anymore. I feel a blackness coming over my heart that I've never known. I feel darker, like I have a sharper edge and a sterner disposition. The magical levity of dryad magic has left me and I'm someone I don't even recognize. I'm different.

"Okay," I say. "Take it away…"

Harlow looks up, brown curls draped over his forehead. We lock eyes, and I can tell he's holding something powerful back. Even as we face each other, I can feel the hum of his power, the buzz of his strength as it surrounds me. And I understand what he's saying, what he's asking.

He can take my pain away by having sex with me. Beyond that, though, I'm not sure. Will the memories return? I could ask him, but I find I don't want to. I don't want to know the answer. All I can focus on, all I can think about is the small bit of respite he's offering me now.

Harlow and I have always been close—maybe he and I were the closest before I left for the Academy of Enchantment. And I've always been attracted to him. We've flirted and kissed and touched before, but we've never taken things further than that. And now?

Now that's what he's asking me, and I realize what my answer is.

"Harlow?" I ask in a small voice. "I want you to take the pain away."

"Are you sure?" he asks. "There's no going back after this, Everly…"

"What do you mean?" I ask quietly. My voice almost shakes.

"I know you're still a virgin."

"I don't care," I answer. And that's the truth—I don't care. Right now, I just want to feel something other than what I'm feeling. I want to lose myself in Harlow, in his body, in the things he can do to my body.

"We can't… we can't do this here," he says as he looks around and I suddenly remember where I am, where we are—Jean-Claude's castle.

He's right—we can't do this here.

"Hold on to me," he says as he wraps his arms around me and carrying me to the window, he wastes no time in leaping out of it as his invisible wings flutter forth and soon we're flying—heading towards his room at Ever Dark Academy.

###

Harlow stares into my eyes and says nothing as he pulls his gloves off. I watch him and swallow hard. Then he moves his hands down the line of my body and when he reaches the hemline of my yoga pants, he hooks his fingers within them and simply peels them down my legs.

His naked touch against my skin causes a flurry of butterflies inside my stomach and my heart immediately starts racing. I gasp and grab the collar of his leather jacket as he pulls me onto his lap. I can immediately feel the hardness of his erection against my hip. He reaches down to my bare sex and, without a word, shoves a finger inside me as I buck in response. I'm already wet, so his manipulation doesn't hurt. No, it feels incredible. Beyond incredible.

He begins to move his finger in and out of me, locking his other arm around my hip, and grinds me hard against him. I can barely breathe. I whimper in his arms, but he doesn't let up.

"Harlow…"

He growls then bucks against me, growing harder through his jeans. The friction is almost burning. I throw my arms around his neck to stop myself from bobbing up and down, and his mouth comes down against mine with bruising pressure. He moans again, this one muffled by my own lips.

Harlow pulls his finger out of me and then presses his large thumb against my sensitive nub at the top of my sex. He rubs me then in small, fervent circles, sending me careening into his chest as I moan with pleasure.

"From the moment I laid eyes on you," he says in a gruff tone. "I've wanted you, and from the moment I spoke to you, I knew I needed to make you mine." He speaks the words like a gentle caress, though his touch is anything but gentle.

"Harlow..." I can barely breathe, can hardly form words because the feel of him, his touch, his kiss, his finger rubbing me in tight little circles. It's almost all too much. I know he's feeding on me, absorbing my life force through my skin, through our contact, but I don't care. I trust him. I know he would never hurt me.

He continues to stare at me and, reaching up, grips my jaw tightly in one large hand. "I'm not a quick fuck to get Griim out of your system," he says, his voice deep and low, but his tone is stern.

"I would never," I start, but he shakes his head to signify that he isn't finished speaking.

"I want to be your forever, Everly. Do you understand?"

"I... I do." What am I saying? I don't know and strangely, I don't care. Whatever he says, I'll agree with it—if only to get him to stop talking. I don't want talking. I want him inside me.

Despite my lingering feelings for Griim and my unutterable heartbreak, I do want Harlow badly. And this isn't a new development. It's always been like this between us. I don't know whether he's rousing these feelings in my body with magic, or with love, but I don't care. I don't care about anything, none of it. All I can care about is this— right here and right now. The feel of him.

"Good," Harlow says.

He smiles down at me and then unzips his pants. He takes out his erection, and wraps my hand around it in a single fluid motion.

"Oh..." I'm stunned by its warmth, the velvety smoothness of his skin. Despite my surprise, I don't let go. "I..." I swallow my fears about the fact that I'm totally new to this, that I've never been in this situation before. "I don't know what to do..."

"Trust your instincts," he says.

He thrusts his hips up and moves his erection up and down against my hand. I stroke him gently, and he moans, a thick, guttural sound I've never heard from any man before. I can feel my need increasing as I watch the effect I have on him— how I can manipulate him into feeling pleasure just like he did to me.

"That's right," he says softly. "Just like that..."

As I pump my hand against him, he grabs onto my thighs and spreads them. His mouth finds mine, and his body pushes me back into the bed. My head hits the pillow, and the hardness of his erection presses firmly against my crotch.

I was never versed in the way of love. I don't know how to please a man or how to receive pleasure in turn. I've only ever known what passed between Jean-Claude and me... Yet, at the thought of facing the pain of losing Griim again... No, I have no other choice but to do this—to numb myself. It's either this or the pain, and I can't take the pain anymore.

Harlow grinds against me. I thrust my hips up to him in answer. His eyes widen a touch in surprise, then a grin spreads across his face. He kisses me deeply, inhaling through his nose.

He thrusts his tongue down my throat and, in response, I throw my arms around his neck and pull him closer. There isn't a whisper of air between us.

While running his hands up and down the length of my body, he licks and bites and sucks and nibbles. He stops with one hand at my waist and the other on my right breast. He squeezes it, kneads it like dough beneath his skillful fingers. He tweaks my nipple, and I cry out.

"That's right…" he moans into my ear.

I feel a probing warmth between my legs. He reaches down and rests his erection at the crux of my opening. I can hardly breathe. Harlow locks eyes with me.

He grabs my hair with both hands and plunges into me.

"Gah!" I grab his shoulders against the sudden sharp and biting pain—I'm not expecting this and it doesn't feel… good. At all. It hurts. "Harlow…"

But as soon as he pushes in fully and then pulls out again, the pain leaves. And in its place is the same bliss I felt before only the feelings are so much stronger now, thicker. He thrusts in and out of me faster and harder, spurred by the sound of me saying his name. The forceful rhythm of his powerful hips forces me into the bed. The sight of his face in the throes of passion is the most arousing thing I've ever seen. I latch my arms around his neck and return the motion of his hips, thrust for thrust. The pleasure building between my legs is too much to contain. I arch tightly against him and scream.

"Goddess!" I cry.

Chest heaving, I fall back against the pillow, but Harlow doesn't let up. I'm spurred on, again, and again, and again.

By the time he finally drops the entirety of his weight on me, his erection still pulsing inside me, I can hear the early morning song of the lark outside my window. Through blurry eyes, I watch the sunrise over Harlow's bare shoulder, and then I let the sweet pull of sleep take me under.

FIFTEEN
♀♥♂♂♂♂
Everly

I feel beaten raw.

My limbs are jelly, and my stomach is in knots.

My first effort to move is a slight shift of my leg. I feel the pain in my body like a rod of lightning through my stomach. Like I've been beaten senseless and then left for dead. Or something like that.

Yet, when I think of last night, my memories are nothing but joyous, if a little conflicted around the edges.

"Goddess..." I mutter.

I catch sight of the large arm that rests above the comforter.

I realize it isn't Griim's, and my heart breaks all over again. I almost cry out in pain, but I'm too weak to even make a sound.

Griim... I see his face too clearly in my mind's eye. His floppy gray hair. His singularly gorgeous golden eyes. His fire...

A single tear tracks down my cheek and lands on my pillow. I wipe away the moisture left in its wake and rub the sleep from my eyes. Gingerly, I lift the comforter and slip out of the bed. I keep my eyes on Harlow's peacefully sleeping face all the while, careful not to wake him. I want a moment to myself before I have to face the reality of what I did last night. What *we* did last night.

Slowly, I pad across the floor on my bare feet toward the bathroom attached to his bedroom. It's a brief but agonizing walk as the floorboard creaks steadfastly under every shift of my weight. Still, Harlow sleeps through it like a champion, hardly moving or altering his snoring pattern in response to the sound.

I reach the small restroom and shut myself inside.

I lean my forehead against the door and sigh.

What a fucking night.

The loss of Griim still hangs heavy in my bones. So, the relief of the pain Harlow offered me was just limited to the time we were together. I understand that now and part of me wishes he could have taken all the pain and the memories away.

I can feel the absence of Griim everywhere, with every breath I take. It's agony, but at the same time, with everything that's been taken away from me... at least there's Harlow. And there's Jean-Claude. Oh, Goddess, Jean-Claude...

I can't imagine it's going to go over well when Jean-Claude learns about Harlow and me.

Why does he have to know? I ask myself.

In all honesty, that's somewhat beside the point. I still haven't figured out what to think about this whole ordeal yet. And the guilt... yes, there's definitely guilt there to deal with too.

How devastated can I really be for Griim if I immediately found comfort in Harlow? I do feel like I've betrayed Griim, but how much can any woman really betray a dead man?

The fact that Griim is really gone is refusing to solidify in my mind. It can't be true. It's too easy. Too simple. Death is just too cruel a fate for such a caring man, and yet, here I find myself.

I put my hand over my mouth and weep over the sink.

I sob, but I'm careful not to make too much noise.

"Get a grip on yourself, Stillwater," I say to the granite counter tops, still looking down at my hands. They look whiter than normal. In fact, all of me is pale.

I grip the sides of the sink with both hands as I inhale a deep, cleansing breath. I wonder briefly if I should use some magic to steady myself, but Mother always told me it was a cheat to use magic when it wasn't necessary.

There's an empty glass by the sink.

I take it in both hands and look through the clear glass. Straight through to the skin of my hand. I see the lines of my palm so clearly magnified. There were lessons on palmistry at the Academy of Divination, but I was never particularly gifted in that arena. My specialty was always casting. It was never divining the future.

And right now, the future is just about the last thing I want to think about. Of course, the past and the present aren't all that hunky-dory either.

I sigh deeply and run my hands over my face.

Then I turn on the sink and fill the glass halfway. I guzzle down the water and refill it, drinking again. I set the glass down then and splash some water on my cheeks, leaving the faucet running as I lose myself to the sound. It isn't much. But it's better than silence. Better than my thoughts.

Just me and the running water. As it should be.

I look up.

I see myself.

I drop the glass in shock.

It shatters on the ground like a crack of lightning. I can't tear my eyes away from my reflection.

Harlow runs into the bathroom, no doubt awakened by the shattering of glass.

"Everly, what's the matter?" He bursts in, worry written in the lines on his handsome face. His curly brown hair is unkempt and matted with sleep. He has the slightest bags under his eyes. In any other circumstances, I would've taken the time to notice how adorable he looks. As it is, I can't notice anything but my own eyes.

"Everly?" The panic in his voice rises.

Rather than answer him, I simply look away from the mirror and stare at him straight in the face.

His eyes go perfectly round.

His mouth falls open.

"Everly..." he says, the shock clear in his voice. "Your eyes..."

"I know," I say barely above a whimper. "I know."

I stare down at the sink again and pinch my wretched eyes shut. Why? Because they're no longer lavender. They're as black as night.

"This can't be happening," I mutter to myself. "This just isn't possible. It just can't be. It isn't true." Yet, I know it's true because the truth is facing me in the mirror.

"Everly!"

Harlow sprints over to me, grabs me by both shoulders, and gives me a shake. He pushes my hair out of my face and tucks it behind my ears. He's looking at me with such loving tenderness, I almost snap.

"What does it mean?" he asks.

I'm silent. I don't even know how to start. Despite knowing the truth, it seems too big a revelation to saddle someone with a six forty-five in the goddamned morning.

"Everly," Harlow says firmly.

He takes such care with the saying of my name, like it's sacred or something. It makes me feel like more than I am. And I'm grateful for that. I need it right now. Now, when I've never felt weaker and more confused.

The height difference between us makes me crane my neck to look up at him. He's well over six feet tall, and I'm much smaller.

I whimper and let out a small sob.

His face changes instantly.

"Everly, please don't cry," he says, desperately wiping tears off my face with his hands. "Look, I'm sure whatever it is that made your eyes go black… we can fix it! Okay? We'll figure it out. We always do. But, for the record, you look just as beautiful now as you ever have."

It's the right thing to say, almost the perfect thing, actually. Still, he doesn't understand, and he won't until I say something. But am I ready?

I guess there's only one way to find out, I think.

He says my name again, soft and slow.

There's something about the tone of his voice, the slight desperation there, that makes me answer him.

"I think… I think either you absorbed too much of me or I've absorbed too much of you," I answer.

Even as I say the words, I can feel the darkness suffusing me, filling me up with feelings that aren't my own, with feelings no dryad should ever feel.

The End

~~~~~~~

To Be Continued In
GOT IT BAD
COMING SOON!
~~~~~~~

H. P. Mallory is a New York Times and
USA Today Bestselling Author!

She lives in Southern California with her son,
where she is at work on her next book.

ALSO BY HP MALLORY:

PARANOMAL WOMEN'S FICTION:
Haven Hollow
Midlife Mermaid
Midlife Spirits

PARANORMAL ROMANCE:
The Underworld Series
Arctic Wolves
Wolves of Valhalla
Lucy Westenra

EPIC FANTASY ROMANCE:
Lily Harper
Dulcie O'Neil
Here to There

PARANORMAL ADVENTURE:
Chasing Demons
Dungeon Raider

REVERSE HAREM:
My Five Kings
Happily Never After

DETECTIVE SCI-FI ROMANCE:
The Alaskan Detective